## "I wasn't going to force myself on you."

"Force yourself on me? What a silly idea!"

"Exactly." Gray eyes glittered down at her, saying they knew just what was the matter.

To save herself, to hang on to the cool "woman of the world" image she had cultivated for so long, Liz used the first thing that came to mind. "I'm still a bit off balance...."

"How long do you need?" Jean-Marc's mouth curved into an understanding smile.

It was the smile that did it. He thought she'd be an easy conquest. Words bubbled onto her tongue and trickled off. "About a couple of weeks," she murmured, a trace of flirtation in her voice. "In fact, by the time my car's repaired, I shall be in a state where I can cope with almost anything."

These books may be available at your local bookseller.

For a list of all titles currently available,
send your name and address to:

Harlequin Reader Service
P.O. Box 52040, Phoenix, AZ 85072-2040
Canadian address: P.O. Box 2800, Postal Station A,
5170 Yonge St., Willowdale, Ont. M2N 5T5

# JENETH MURREY

## double doubting

*Harlequin Books*

TORONTO • NEW YORK • LONDON
AMSTERDAM • PARIS • SYDNEY • HAMBURG
STOCKHOLM • ATHENS • TOKYO • MILAN

Harlequin Presents first edition December 1984
ISBN 0-373-10748-X

Original hardcover edition published in 1984
by Mills & Boon Limited

# CHAPTER ONE

'THIS torch is going out, I can hardly see by it,' twelve-year-old Hamish Mackenzie sounded aggrieved. 'Liz,' he enquired of his aunt, 'what shall we do if it dies on us before we get there?'

Liz Fellowes pushed a lock of blonde hair from her forehead, took a firmer grasp of the steering wheel and screwed up her very blue eyes to peer out through the windscreen into the wild, windswept darkness. 'We stop,' she announced calmly. 'We pull in to the side of the road, put on the interior light and try to discover where you've landed us this time.' Some of her calm deserted her. 'You and your route!' she snapped.

'We should have had a bigger torch,' Ham lamented.

'We did—oh, we did; until you left it behind in Pont Audemer,' Liz took a hold on her temper. 'Oh, for crying out loud!' as the Mini Traveller shook every nut and bolt bouncing over a pothole. 'I thought you said this was a minor road? It's a cart track! Are you sure we're where we're supposed to be? I've this horrible feeling we're lost again, and an even worse feeling that I'll never see Avignon.'

Avignon, the very name was like a talisman—for a split second she could see it: the deep blue of the sky, the blazing sun shining down on Bev's bronzed shoulders, sparkling on the hairs of his chest and turning his rough fair hair to silver—the gay little orange and blue tent against the brown of the parched grass—The Mini lurched over another pothole and she came back

5

to the present, to a wet night in the Loire valley, a howling, gale-force wind that lashed the rain into the windscreen and to the deepening certainty that she had been the biggest fool in creation when she had allowed herself to be bulldozed into bringing her nephew to stay with his French pen-friend.

'We're here! We've arrived! I can see it!' Ham was bouncing with excitement. 'Look, Liz, over on the right, can't you see?'

'See what?' Liz said grumpily. 'I can hardly see the road. Stop bouncing about like a wild thing and tell me what I'm supposed to be looking for.'

'The gates!' Ham was almost shouting. 'Louis said there were these enormous gates, and they must be just as huge as he said, I can see the pillars—they've got things stuck on the top of them, I wonder what they are?'

'Busts of Napoleon?' Liz said sarcastically. 'It's a favourite form of decoration in France.'

'Turn right, turn right—Here—oh, Liz, you're going to miss them! Oh no, you haven't,' as the tires crunched on gravel. 'Liz, do you think it's one of those chateau places—you *will* stay with me for a couple of days, won't you? Mum said you would—just while I get used to things.'

Stay with him? Liz felt her blood pressure rising. Already she'd added nearly a hundred and forty miles to her journey, had to change her Channel crossing, gone miles out of her way. She should have been in Avignon by now, not wandering through this murk, looking for one house on a cart track to nowhere. The surface of the drive was much smoother than that of the road they'd just left, and unconsciously, her foot went down on the accelerator. Avignon—she supposed she could manage a day with Ham, see what this French family was like, make sure he would be happy with them—Marcie would want a full report. Just a day, not any more than that. . . .

'Liz! Stop!' Ham was literally screaming in her ear. 'Stop! You're going to hit it!' and she did. What she had taken for a darker shadow among all the other shadows cast by the headlights was, in reality, a tree, lying across the drive, where no tree should be. Her foot shifted to the brake, but she was too late, she knew it as the wheels locked and the little Traveller skidded. She felt the crash as the bonnet rammed into the tree-trunk and in slow motion, she watched the steering wheel come towards her face. Bev's car, she thought dully as her hand went out to switch off the ignition. Bev's car— not new, over ten years old, but he'd been so proud of it. The steering wheel cracked against her temple and she moaned with pain and shock, and then everything was quiet with only the sound of the rain spattering on the roof; even the wind seemed to have died and Ham wasn't shouting any more.

Slowly, Liz raised her head from where it was resting on the wheel; it felt as if every bone in her neck and shoulders had been cracked and displaced. 'Ham,' she almost groaned the name. 'Are you all right?'

''Course I am,' but there was a quaver in his voice. She felt him wriggling about and then, 'No bones broken and no blood. How're you?'

'Alive,' she made it sound cheerful and a bit jokey. 'Are we anywhere near the house? Can you see a light?'

'It can't be very far away.' She heard the click as he undid his safety-belt and another as he fumbled at his door-lock. 'I say, isn't this super!' Apparently it took more than a car crash to dampen Ham's enthusiasm. 'I mean, the ferry, that hotel in Pont Audemer and getting lost outside Angers—and now this! I'll have something to tell the boys at school when I get back! I bet none of them have had such a good time. Are you coming, Liz? We'll have to walk the rest of the way, but it can't be far.'

'You didn't say anything about climbing over a damn great tree,' Liz protested as she skidded on the rough bark. 'This thing's covered with slimy stuff, I'm going to get filthy. Drat you!' as she slipped again. 'I'm not going a step further, I'm soaked. Go on up to the house and bring me a stretcher—I feel awful!'

'You *did* hurt yourself?' Ham summoned up a bit of concern. 'O.K., you wait here, I won't be long,' and he scampered off into the darkness which closed in behind him, leaving her alone. With a moan, she dropped her head in her filthy hands. She felt sick, her teeth were beginning to chatter and she was shaking all over, and the rain wasn't helping. Already, she was soaked through to the skin and her jeans and tee-shirt were clinging to her like a second skin. All she could think about was Marcie, her dear, dratted sister who had engineered this foul-up. If it hadn't been for Marcie. . . . Liz closed her eyes and she was back in the kitchen of the house where she had been born. Marcie lived there now, and Marcie was making tarts. The kitchen was unbearably hot and Marcie was red with wrath.

'You could do it if you wanted to,' she slammed the rolling pin down and grabbed at the pastry cutter. 'Your trouble is that you've gone damn selfish since Bev was killed. You won't think of anybody but yourself! I know you've had it bad, but that's no reason for shutting yourself away, never coming to see us unless I send for you. Anybody'd think it was a thousand miles from your flat in Paddington to Richmond!'

Liz tried to shut it out, to concentrate on immediates, but the scene continued, like a flickering re-run of an old movie; she could see the baking trays ready on the table, hear herself speaking.

'I'll take him as far as Paris,' she offered reluctantly. 'I'll put him on the right train at the Gare d'Austerlitz and I'll phone so somebody will meet him at the other end.'

'Not good enough!' Marcie was cutting out pastry circles with the speed born of long practice. 'You can take him all the way; it's no skin off your nose, and it isn't often I ask a favour. You're my sister and Ham's your nephew!' Marcie never pleaded, she stormed, getting rattier with every frustrated moment. 'I know it's a bit out of your way. . . .'

'A bit! Three hundred miles is a bit? And that's what it will be on the round trip, delivering him and then picking him up.'

The movie stopped running as Liz heard Ham's excited treble. '*Notre auto est* smashed to bits and *ma tante*, my aunt, you know, *elle* has hit her *tête* on the steering wheel!' Liz smiled reluctantly. Ham would never be a linguist and she hoped whoever was with him could speak English. Her own French was good, but she was too tired, too sick to bother. There was a slithering sound and a thump as somebody climbed over the tree to land beside her.

'You're hurt, *madame*?' A torch shone brightly in her face and she winced away from the light and shut her eyes.

'Yes!' she growled ungraciously, 'and I'm going to be sick!' Her thoughts were coming slowly now, and as they came, she uttered them aloud. 'I can't climb over that tree—You've no business to have a tree across your drive, it's dangerous—I don't think I'll ever get to Avignon—I'm fated!' She thought she was crying, but with the rain streaming down her face, dripping from her hair, she couldn't be sure, and when a firm hand took her chin and forced her face round and into the torch beam she kept her eyelids tight shut. 'Oh lord, but I'm tired!'

The voice that broke in on her thoughts was deep and quiet, hardly French at all, with only a very slight slurring of the syllables to mar the excellent English. 'Of course, *madame*, you've travelled a long way. No,' as she struggled to rise, 'I'll carry you; it isn't far. *Soyez tranquille, petite*, soon you shall be dry and warm, and fortunately, the doctor's dined with me tonight. He'll mend any little damage.'

'I can't get over that tree,' Liz explained gravely, still confused.

'No need,' and the voice altered to a brisk tone. 'Take the torch, Ham, and walk beside me—no, don't bother about the cases, someone will fetch them later.'

It was good to have someone's arms about her. Liz moved her cheek against fine cloth, soft and plushy—velvet? It had been so long since she'd had the comfort of Bev's arms—too long. Three weary cold years, and now, her tears came in earnest, trickling salty into her mouth so that she turned her face into the jacket when at last she was in the warmth of the house—hiding her face and her grief from prying eyes. She was put down on a couch and there was the chill slipperiness of satin under her head. The sickness had vanished and she started to come to life, opening her eyes to a huge room, lit only by a few dim lamps and the glow from a wide, deep fireplace. The calm deep voice switched from English to French.

'Marie-France, fetch your father from where he is in the kitchen with Berthe and pray she hasn't blinded him with her Calvados. Tell him there's been an accident— Ah, Louis, your friend has arrived, but go instantly and tell Henri to bring in the *valises* from the car in the drive. After that, bring me a bowl of water and a sponge. Tell Henri to be careful, the wind has brought a tree down across the drive.'

Liz gazed round at cream and gold walls, dark old portraits and exquisite but stiff furnishings. Louis Quinze, her mind registered that—gold, curly legs and satin upholstery—if the couch she was lying on was anything to go by, it was damned uncomfortable to sit on; and then the girl Marie-France was back, not a day over seventeen and trying to look ten years older than her age. Red-gold hair and a green evening gown—too décolleté, too slinky—poor kid, Liz wondered who she was trying to attract. She could see Ham in the background, his face white with shock and exhaustion and his red hair all over the place, and then there were two other faces peering down at her, and she gasped.

The young Lucifer, black-haired, dark-eyed, looking at her from a Botticelli angel face, and beside it, the same face, only much older. Lucifer fallen—the same black hair, the same dark eyes, even the face was the same, but different. This older one was marred, ruined with a deep hellish disillusion. Under the black arching brows, the dark eyes were hooded beneath heavy lids thickly fringed with feminine lashes, and the mouth had an almost sneering curve as though the eyes had seen too much. The young, dark angel gave her a sweet smile as his elder counterpart spoke.

'Jean-Marc St Clair at your service, *madame*. Welcome to Dieudonné—and this is Louis,' and then he was back to French again with a speed and ease which took her breath away. 'Louis, tell Berthe to warm the bed for Madame and ask Monsieur le Docteur to hurry. He may return to Berthe and the Calvados when he has attended to Madame's hurts.'

The child hitched the belt of his very chic French pyjamas a little higher and scampered off out of her view, while Liz at last found her tongue.

'I'm glad to meet you,' she was aggressively English. 'I'm Mrs Fellowes, Ham's aunt. His mother, my sister, couldn't come, so I brought him. I'm on my way to Avignon.' The thought of the little green Traveller with its bonnet buried in a tree upset her new-found confidence. 'Do you know if my car's badly damaged—it's most important I push on as quickly as possible.'

Ham's voice rose in the background, a treble howl of anguish. 'Liz, you *promised*! You said you'd stay a while. You promised Mum!'

'No need,' she forced a smile. 'Everybody seems to speak English, you'll be all right, Ham.' It was meant to be comforting, but Jean-Marc St Clair spoiled it.

'I speak English, *madame*, but Louis doesn't and neither does anybody else. But we won't talk about tomorrow until it comes. You need rest, and in the daylight we shall be better able to see what damage you've done to your car. You're meeting somebody in Avignon?'

Dumbly, Liz shook her head, and as a shaft of pain shot through her temple, she wished she hadn't. 'No, *m'sieur*, I'm not meeting anyone,' and she folded her lips firmly. She could have said so much more, all the words were a pain in her chest. There wouldn't be anybody there to meet her, not even a ghost. There would only be memories, and maybe with them, she'd draw nearer to Bev, be able to see his face in her mind's eye once more. Her memory of Bev shouldn't have dulled, misted over so quickly—she had tried to keep it bright and clear, but slowly, over these past three years, he had withdrawn from her, right to the edge of her vision where he was no more than a hazy outline—a dim figure, walking away from her.

'So, you will stay, if only for a few days,' Jean-Marc stroked the hair from her temple and examined the bruising and his finger slid down her cheekbone, stroking the soreness there. 'It doesn't look too bad,' his smile took her breath away. 'I don't think you'll have a black eye.' He turned to the young girl who was at his elbow as though she was tied there with a very short string. 'This is Mademoiselle Marie-France Debret, the daughter of our doctor—and speak of the devil, here he is. Paul, my friend, we have a patient for you.'

Liz submitted to the examination wearily, she blinked when her eyes were peered into closely with the aid of a torch and protested, 'There's nothing wrong with me, honestly. I've just had a little bump on the head. Mostly, I'm tired, I think.' The torch was shone in her eyes again and she winced. 'What's he doing that for?'

'To see if you have concussion,' Jean-Marc said soothingly, and he grasped the hand with which she was attempting to push the doctor away and held it firmly. 'Head injuries can be serious, and I remember you said you felt sick. . . .'

'I don't have concussion!' she said sharply. 'I told you, it's only a little bump, but I'm tired and his light hurts my eyes. I'm not even feeling sick any more—just tired and,' she looked down at the ruin of her jeans and her slime-covered tee-shirt, 'filthy! All I need is a cup of tea, a couple of aspirin, a bath and somewhere to sleep. I'll be as right as rain in the morning.'

'We'll see,' he smiled down at her, and went off into a huddle with the doctor, Marie-France going with him as though she couldn't trust him more than a pace away from her.

Poor kid! Liz felt a tart pity for the girl. So young, so obvious about her teenage crush—and she was wasting her time. Their host seemed to treat her as though she was not much older than his son, despite the too sophisticated dress and the deep plum lipstick on her young, soft mouth. Young love was wonderful; Liz remembered her own. It was also very painful, but she'd been spared that. She and Bev had gone from young love easily into the real, grown-up thing—a quiet, deep emotion where words were hardly necessary and a touch of the fingers or a look was all that was needed for complete communion.

Liz didn't have her aspirin, instead she had a glassful of milky-looking fluid which tasted vile, but she forced it down—she'd had French draughts before and knew that they were as good as, sometimes better than tablets. Her forehead had been painted with a salve, and Ham and Louis together had brought her a cup of tea; all she wanted now was a bath—she must look a sight! And then sleep. She bit back a yawn as she swung herself off the couch and Jean-Marc was at her side.

'Marie-France, you're going to be a nurse, so they tell me. Now you can have your first practice. Take Madame upstairs and show her to her bedroom, it's the one next to Madame St Clair's, and you can help her to take a bath.' It was said, slowly, in English. 'And you can practise your English at the same time.'

'I will not be a nurse,' Marie-France smiled at him dazzlingly while she coped badly with her schoolgirl English. It was heavily accented but quite understandable. 'It is too hard work. I think I will marry a farmer instead,' and the smile became flirtatious. 'Why can't Berthe attend her?'

'Because Berthe is too old and too fat to climb the stairs, *ma petite*. She has also finished her work for today and is enjoying a rest. As for marrying a farmer, that too is very hard work, and it would mean leaving home. All the young farmers around here are married already, all except one, and he is far too old for a young girl like you.'

Liz sighed wearily as she pushed back a heavy lock of her blonde hair and her eyes, blue and bruised with fatigue, hardened. She didn't want any help, especially help so grudgingly given—she could manage quite well by herself.

'Just point me in the right direction,' she appealed cheerfully, 'and I'll be on my way.' Her legs, when she finally stood on them, felt like cotton wool, but she would go by herself, under her own steam, she was determined on it.

Jean-Marc transferred his frown from Marie-France to herself. 'Nonsense, if Marie is in no mood to help, I shall take you myself,' and there was a firm arm about her shoulders, another beneath her knees, and she was lifted and carried out of the room. Liz thought she was being used to show the girl his indifference. She didn't like that—to her, it smacked of cruelty, but there was nothing she could do about it.

She stole a glance up at his face as they mounted the stairs, a face which she found fascinating. And she wondered what hell he'd looked into which had changed him into this travesty of beauty, because despite the bitterness in the sensual curve of his mouth and the weary tolerance in his hooded eyes, he was the most beautiful man she had ever seen. Beautiful and— she searched for the right word and found it—damned! It was there in the flare of his nostrils, in his grey eyes— not, now she could see them properly, as dark as the boy's—and in the smooth curve of his chin, a curve which couldn't hide a fierce determination.

'You've inspected me thoroughly?' He'd caught her at it and she closed her eyes swiftly. 'What's the verdict? Am I responsible enough to have charge of your nephew? Which reminds me, when I've seen to you, I shall phone his mother to let her know you've arrived.'

Liz's reaction was immediate and automatic; her hand grasped his sleeve until her knuckles whitened and her eyes filled with terror.

'You won't say anything about the accident?' she implored. 'My sister's all alone, her husband's on an oil rig in the North Sea and she isn't well, that's why she didn't bring Ham herself. She's going into hospital for a bit of an op, but if she knows about me crashing the car, she'll worry herself sick unless she drops everything and comes flying out here.'

'But Ham's unharmed,' Jean-Marc let loose with his smile. 'I shall tell her so. . . .'

'You could tell her till you're blue in the face, it wouldn't make any difference,' Liz almost wept at his ignorance. 'Ham's Marcie's ewe lamb—the fact that he wasn't hurt has nothing to do with it. Please,' she pleaded, 'don't mention the accident, just say we arrived safely. That's true, isn't it; you wouldn't be telling a lie.'

Jean-Marc's smile became satanic, 'I think I could be

persuaded,' he murmured. 'This sounds to me like a bargain—you want something from me, so let's see what I can extract from you in exchange. Yes, I have it,' and he nodded seriously, seeming to take a great deal of pleasure from her outraged expression. 'You promised both your nephew and his mother you'd stay for a couple of days—it depends of course on how long it will take to repair your car, but I'd like you to stay a little longer than that—say a couple of weeks.'

'Oh no!' Liz was as firm as her aching head would allow. 'I told you, I have to get to Avignon. . . .'

'Avignon—Avignon,' he sighed. 'You're beginning to sound like a damaged record with the needle stuck in one groove. That was practically the first word I heard you say, and you've been repeating it at short intervals ever since. Avignon's been there for nearly a thousand years, it won't vanish in a couple of weeks. Do we have a bargain—er—Liz? That's what Ham calls you, and it suits you better than Madame Fellowes, so I'll make myself free of it—and you may call me Jean-Marc,' he added generously.

Liz's eyes sparkled. She was fighting for something; she didn't quite know if it was worth fighting for, but it was the first time in three years that she'd had the inclination to do anything except close her eyes and let the world go by. 'I don't think I like you very much, *m'sieur*,' she scolded.

'Jean-Marc,' he corrected innocently. 'We'd agreed on that, if you remember—and I promise you something. At the end of two weeks, you won't dislike me at all. I'm a very likeable person.'

They had reached the door of her room and he pushed it open with his foot, entered and set her down on her feet. 'Now, are we agreed, Liz?'

She shook her head; every vertebra in her neck protested, but the pain was welcome—Jean-Marc had a soothing voice when he chose and she could feel herself being persuaded—almost. 'I think I'd like to see and speak to Madame St Clair first,' she said sedately. 'She might not wish to have another guest foisted on her.'

'Impossible.' Jean-Marc was also sedate. 'Madame St Clair lives in Paris and she and I don't correspond, certainly not about who I entertain in this house.'

A broken marriage. Liz gazed down at the dirty marks her sandals were making on the pink and blue flowers of the carpet and forced her head to do a bit of serious thinking. Marcie had picked up a great deal of narrow-mindedness from her husband, who was the essence of a Scottish Covenanter. A child's home had, of necessity, to contain both parents, otherwise it didn't qualify as a home for a child. Marcie wouldn't like Ham to live in what she would call an irregular establishment and Ian would go up the wall. She, Liz, could be in bigger trouble leaving Ham here than crashing into a tree. The tree episode would be forgotten in time, but this—every time Ham got himself into trouble, Liz would be to blame for leaving him in a house where he might have picked up wrong ideas. If Jean-Marc had been a widower, her sister would have thought nothing of it, but separations and divorce drove Marcie into a steaming rage, especially if there were children of the marriage. She made up her mind.

'Very well, I'll stay for a while. It'll probably take that long to get my car repaired,' she justified herself and her weak-mindedness aloud.

'Good!' He gave her another breathtaking smile. 'Louis and I will make plans for your entertainment—and while I'm on the subject of phone calls, would you like me to ring your husband—if you'll give me the number. . . .'

A number to reach Bev! Liz only wished she had such a thing! The cold loneliness swept over her again, driving the little colour from her face and giving her soft mouth a despondent droop. 'That won't be necessary,' she said.

'But surely you want him to know . . .?'

Liz turned away from him to hide the tears. 'I said it won't be necessary.' It came out on a gruff, defiant tone and she changed the subject. 'Which is the bathroom, please?'

'In there,' he pointed to a door in the wall opposite the bed. 'I'll allow you fifteen minutes, and then you must be in bed,' he gestured to where her case was sitting on the top of a delicate marquetry table. 'I've had your things brought up and there's everything you require in the bathroom. No longer than fifteen minutes,' he reminded her. 'Our doctor's medicines are powerful and I wouldn't like you to fall asleep in the bath.'

When he had gone, Liz tumbled through her caseful of clothing to find a fresh cotton nightie, and armed with that and her toilet bag, she went off to the bathroom. Really—she gazed round at expensive tiling, wall mirrors and gold-plated taps—Ham hadn't been far wrong when he'd asked if this house could be a chateau. It wasn't, of course—from what she had seen, it was far too small, but it was the acme of luxury and an expensive taste; a showpiece—no, she corrected herself, a showcase furnished as a setting for somebody—perhaps the absent Madame St Clair. Any further thoughts were driven clean out of her head when she caught sight of herself in one of the mirrored panels on the wall. Her reflection did more than anything else to pull her together. She was filthy from head to toe, her hair hung about her face, unkempt and witchlike, and her face! It was quite colourless, her eyes looked like holes burned in a blanket and the bruising on her temple and cheekbone was an angry red which threatened to turn to all the colours of the rainbow. Not an inviting sight!

She grinned wryly to herself as she stepped into the hot scented water. Maybe it would be better to stay here until she could show her usual appearance to the world at large. There was also the question of her car and how long it would take to repair. Liz felt perspiration—nothing to do with the heat of the bathwater—dew her forehead as she realised she was blithely assuming the car *could* be repaired. Perhaps it was a complete write-off, she could be stranded here for the whole holiday—but somehow, that wasn't such a frightening thought after all. She was aware of a warm, cosy lethargy stealing over her, relaxing every taut nerve and muscle. The doctor's filthy medicine—it might be wiser not to take any chances. Jean-Marc St Clair had done enough already, the last thing she wanted was for him to have to haul her naked body from a bath.

Her hands wouldn't work properly, the towel was too big, too fluffy, and it kept slipping out of her fingers, so she slid her still wet body into her nightie and walked slowly and deliberately across to the bed.

Ham and Louis paid her a visit just as she had slipped between the sheets, Louis still chic in his navy pyjamas piped with white and Ham more soberly clad in striped cotton.

'Jean-Marc says it's all right.' Ham had evidently succumbed to the St Clair charm, he only had to mention the name and his eyes went glassy with devotion. 'He said he'd "prevailed on you to extend your stay". And he's phoned Mum. He's a brick, Liz, he didn't say a word about the accident and I said to tell Mum I was fast asleep in bed because you know what she's like. She asks all sorts of questions, and before you know it, I've spilled the beans.'

Louis stood shyly in the background until Ham gave him a fierce nod and a bit of a shove. 'Say what I told you,' he directed in a loud stage whisper, and Louis advanced to put a small hand on her cheek before he consulted a grubby piece of paper, reading from it aloud.

'I am pleased you are staying, Madame Liz, and I will try to make you 'appy.' Liz waited for more, but nothing came. Louis had evidently practised this little speech and she'd get nothing until he'd practised some more.

The boys went off, and her next visitor was Jean-Marc with a large bowl of chocolate. He looked not uncomfortable but faintly regretful as, without asking, he seated himself on the edge of her bed.

'Liz, you will have to forgive me, but I thought I was acting in your best interests. You refused me your husband's phone number and you were strange about it. I thought there was possibly something wrong, that you might have quarreled, even separated, so I asked Ham if he knew it.'

'And Ham told you . . .?'

'. . . That he was killed three years ago, yes.'

Liz shrugged, the drug making her careless of consequences. 'Anybody can get anything out of Ham, he has a wagging tongue. That's why he wouldn't speak to his mother. But you needn't fear you've upset me, it all happened a long time ago, so I shan't weep all over the place. As a matter of fact,' she was a bit defiant, 'I'm very well adjusted—what you'd call a merry widow.' She drained the bowlful of chocolate and closed her eyes. 'I'd like to sleep now, if that's all right with you. Any further personal questions can wait until tomorrow, I'm sure, and tomorrow I'll feel better, I hope. Well enough to tell you to mind your own damn business! But don't let anything spoil your fun, please. A married woman on the loose or a widow, there's not much difference between them, they're both fair game. That's one thing I've learned!'

Perhaps she hadn't really said it aloud, she couldn't be sure. Jean-Marc gave nothing away and he didn't attempt to reply. Instead, he leaned closer over her and his finger touched her ear.

'Did you know you've lost an earring?'

This brought her bolt upright, fighting against the stupor that threatened to overwhelm her. 'My earring? Oh no!' Her hand went to her left ear where the little gold Tudor rose with a single small pearl at its centre still swung, but on her right ear there was nothing except a tiny soreness where the hook had been torn from the lobe. 'I must find it,' she struggled to get out from the hampering sheets. 'Perhaps it's in the bath— caught up in the towel. . . .'

'. . . Lying on the floor of your car or dropped somewhere by the tree,' he suggested, 'even fallen off along the drive. No, Liz, you can't search at this time of night, not when you're full of a sedative. Lie back.' His hands were firm on her shoulders, pushing her back against the pillows and she couldn't fight him.

'Damn you to hell!' she gasped in impotent fury and grief.

'Hell, Liz?' she could hardly see his face through the fog before her eyes, but she could hear the pain in his voice. 'I've been there, *mignonne,* and I wouldn't send my worst enemy to that place. Go to sleep, we'll have a search in the morning,' and suddenly, Bev was with her, his arms about her, drawing her close and pressing her head against his chest while he wiped away her tears with a handkerchief which smelled of a strange cologne, and she relaxed against him. Everything would be all right now.

'It's been such a long time,' she told him sadly, and felt his mouth on hers as she drifted away into a dark nothingness.

# CHAPTER TWO

SOMETHING like a minor eruption woke Liz and she opened a reluctant eye to see first Louis, carefully shutting the bedroom door, and then, as she swivelled her head on a neck which felt as though it had been put through a mangle, there was Ham at the long window, wrestling with the louvred shutters.

'Can't you do anything quietly?' she complained as, after a lot of grunting and puffing, they swung open. 'You sound like an earthquake! It's no wonder your mum's nerves are in tatters!'

'Sorry, Liz.' Ham came to the side of the bed in an exaggerated tiptoe creep and she glared at him crossly.

'It's too late for that now, the damage is done; you've woken me up!' Both boys had towels draped about their necks and she roused herself to take a little interest.

'Where are you off to?' she demanded querulously. 'No, don't tell me if you don't want to; let me worry!' Her eyes slid to Louis, who seemed to be happier in the background. *Bonjour*, Louis, *comment ça va?*'

Louis' face lighted up with an angelic smile of relief and he hastened into an involved explanation, the gist of which was that he had lent Ham a bike and they were both going to Villiers where there was a *piscine* and an instructor who would give them lessons. He finished off in English, another lesson thoroughly learned, 'I am ver' huh-appy,' he aspirated like mad, 'and I huh-ope you are better.'

Ham took over when Louis dried up. 'We've been up

for *hours*—and we've been down to the farm for the milk and had our breakfasts and everything. It's a shame you can't come with us, Louis said you could have borrowed Berthe's bike, but Jean-Marc says the doctor's coming, so you won't be able to.'

'Grrr!' Liz showed her teeth at him. 'After what I went through yesterday, I'm not moving more than a few yards in any direction today—in fact, I don't think I'll move at all.' She became serious. 'My car, Ham— and have you looked for my earring?'

'Mmm,' Ham nodded. 'We've been up and down the drive, but we couldn't find it. Louis says when we get back from the *piscine*, he'll get out his metal detector and we'll try again. We couldn't look in the car because Jean-Marc's had it towed away, he said the sight of it would send you into hysterics. He's had the tree towed away as well. Well,' he grasped Louis' arm in a determined fashion, 'we'll have to be off now—ta-ta, see you at lunch time!' and Liz was left, staring at the panels of the door and wondering what she'd done to be treated in such a cavalier fashion. Not one enquiry as to her health or wellbeing—Ham hadn't even asked if she'd slept well!

The short walk to the bathroom made her breathless and she was glad to sink down on to the stool, closing her eyes until things steadied—but that, she reasoned, had little to do with the bump to her head. It was probably the after-effects of the medicine and it would pass, and after a cool shower, during which she washed her hair free of the tiny pieces of dead leaves and moss which were stuck in it, Liz sorted out a clean pair of jeans and a fresh tee-shirt, together with fresh underwear, for the benefit not only of the doctor but her own self-esteem.

She was good-looking and she knew it, but she had few affectations, in fact those good looks had caused her a lot of trouble over the past three years, and nowadays she did her best to tone them down. She pulled her still wet hair back ruthlessly into a ponytail when she had dressed and crossed to the dressing-table mirror to check that she was neat and nothing of the battered, muddy Liz of last night remained—but the mirror gave the lie to her hopes. Her face was still paper-white and the bruising looked angry, as though she'd been in a fist fight, and with a sigh of despair she slackened the leather buckle which held her hair and pulled forward a heavy swathe to cover her high forehead, pushing it back into its natural wave with her fingers. She nodded with satisfaction at the result, she had covered the ugly bruise very well—and then pondered the discoloration on her cheekbone. Something to cover that, make-up wouldn't do, but she felt in her shoulder bag and dragged out the sunglasses she had bought for the journey—very big, dark lenses which wrapped round and did a splendid job of camouflage. She was just pushing her feet into a pair of unsullied sneakers when there was a soft tap on the door and she swung round from her case to see Jean-Marc entering with a tray.

'Good morning, Liz,' his eyes slid over her with appreciation in their grey depths. 'I don't care for the spectacles, though, I can't see your eyes and so I don't know what you're thinking. Are they really necessary?'

'Very necessary.' She lifted them fractionally to show her battered cheekbone and dropped them again swiftly. He couldn't see what she was thinking, which was all to the good, an added bonus, in fact. This man saw too much, his eyes would strip her mind naked.

She turned back to the dressing-table and with a gentle finger touched the solitary Tudor rose earring lying on the crystal tray.

'The boys didn't find the other one,' and she couldn't hide the pain in her voice. 'Has anybody looked in the car, because I've been over the bathroom and the towels I used, and it's not there.'

'It's important to you?'

'Yes, very!' She couldn't find the courage to say why, not to tell almost a complete stranger that her aids to memory were so few. The earrings—Bev had bought them for her when they had gone to choose an engagement ring. Nothing expensive, because Bev just didn't have that kind of money, and she had preferred a large, watery green peridot to the small diamond which was all he could afford. The earrings had been bought with the balance of the sum he could afford and she treasured them, together with his watch.

A cool breeze blew in through the open shutters and she shivered, feeling the sting of gooseflesh on her arms, to be back once again on the hillside on the Pennines and standing in the cold wind while Bev sailed above her on wide blue wings. Behind the sunglasses, her eyes closed and she saw once more those wings, the flutter of them, and then the dizzying spiral as the hang-glider plunged to land nearly at her feet, a smashed and tattered blue bird, and Bev smashed with it, his watch the only thing to survive. She had had the wide stainless steel bracelet removed and a thin lizardskin strap put in its place, and she wore it all the time. Much too big for a woman, of course, and it wasn't a sprig of rosemary, but it was remembrance!

She saw Jean-Marc's eyes on her fingers where they were tracing out the wide, time-elapsed bezel which surrounded the watch face, and she forced her lips into a rueful smile—what her eyes were expressing didn't matter; as he said, he couldn't see them. 'Silly of me,' she widened the smile. 'I forgot to put my watch on an hour when we landed in France. It's later than I thought. I was just coming downstairs in search of some real French coffee, the stuff we had yesterday morning at Pont Audemer was disappointing.' She was babbling away, she could hear herself and she couldn't stop. 'Ham said the doctor was coming, but it isn't necessary, you know. I'm as fit as a fiddle.'

'I don't doubt it.' Jean-Marc took the tray across to the table by the window. 'Come and have your coffee, Liz, I've brought an extra bowl in case you invited me to join you.'

Liz had got hold of herself, pushing her memories to the back of her mind. 'Of course,' she said sedately. 'I'll be glad of the company. Ham also said that they couldn't search the car because you'd had it towed away. There was also something about me having hysterics if I saw it . . .?'

He shrugged, a graceful gesture, nothing like an English shrug. 'It's always the same when one crashes a car, the damage always seems to look worse than it really is. I remember the first time it happened to me—it was my father's car, one of those old Citroëns, nearly new at the time, and I looked at it and wondered how it could ever go again. Yours is the same, a lot of superficial damage but nothing that can't be repaired, given time and the spare parts. My mechanic's looked it over and he thinks about two weeks, maybe less if he can get hold of the parts he needs quickly.'

'Two weeks!' Liz took a gulp of coffee. 'But I can't. . . .'

'. . . Which is the length of time you agreed to stay when we spoke last night,' he reminded her. 'Or were you so full of sedative you don't remember? The boys have made plans for your entertainment—only in the afternoons, of course,' he gave her one of his heartbreaking smiles. 'The mornings are to be devoted to swimming. When it comes to a choice between you and a well muscled swimming instructor, I'm afraid you have to take second place. Are you addicted to chateaux?' This stirred Liz's sense of the ridiculous and she choked back a laugh.

'Not much,' she admitted. 'I've seen Chambord, which I think is fantastic—more on the roof than there is in the house itself, if you see what I mean, but after that I went to Versailles and came away with an acute attack of indigestion.'

'A bit too florid for your taste? Never mind, the chateaux in this region are a little more austere. . . .'

'I was thinking,' she interrupted. 'There isn't any real need to wait for my car—a few days and I could easily go by train. . . .'

'Oh no! I'm holding you to your part of our deal—two weeks, and it won't all be chateaux visiting. One evening next week, you'll accompany me to Marie-France's birthday party—a very grand affair in the hotel in Villiers, we're all invited.'

Liz went quiet; she didn't say 'No', she pushed her sun-specs more firmly on to the bridge of her nose and deliberately changed the subject.

'Ham and Louis seem to get on very well together, don't they?' She managed a bright tone. 'I think it's wonderful, considering they neither of them speak the other's language properly—and the age gap,' she hurried on, 'boys of that age make a great deal out of two years, but your son doesn't seem to mind at all when Ham takes the lead . . .'

'My son?' Jean-Marc's mouth curved into a smile and then enlightenment dawned and he chuckled. 'You've got it all wrong, *petite*. As they say in the States, you've got your wires crossed. The Madame St Clair who lives in Paris isn't my wife, she's my stepmother, and Louis is my half-brother.'

He wasn't the only one on whom enlightenment dawned. Liz recalled Marie-France's flirtatious remark of the previous evening. Her mouth tightened as the suspicion came that she was being used.

'And are you by any chance a farmer?' Her nose twitched fastidiously. 'The one that Mademoiselle Debret prefers to marry, rather than be a nurse?'

'Yes,' he was quite shameless. 'That's why I want you with me at the birthday party.'

Liz let her next words come with an Arctic chill. '*Monsieur*, I don't care to be used in that way, neither am I in France to extricate you from the results of your flirting, and,' the chill vanished as she felt herself get heated, 'although I'll stay here for a while—I don't like to break promises which you've made on my behalf to children—I shan't be going to any birthday party.' The heat grew and she ceased to be polite. 'If you've got yourself into a pickle because you've encouraged a teenage girl, you can damn well get out of it yourself! I'm not going to help you! I've enough problems of my own without coping with your self-inflicted ones.'

'And, my dear *madame*,' Jean-Marc leaned back in his chair and copied her snooty tone exactly, 'I don't truly require any help to deal with a teenage girl—I could manage half a dozen with my hands tied behind my back, but I don't care to hurt people, especially somebody as young and vulnerable as Marie-France.'

'Then why,' Liz snapped it out, 'why didn't you start the discouraging process a bit earlier, if you're so good at it?—or did it give your ego a kick to have a young girl swooning at your feet? You look about thirty-five to me, which means you're quite old enough to recognise the signs—you've probably led her on. . . .'

'*Stupide!*' He was as incensed as she was. 'I didn't recognise the signs, as you call it, because I wasn't looking for them. To me, she's always been a child, I've never thought of her in any other way—that is, until last night when she invited herself to dinner and tripped in dressed in that awful get-up. Now, I want to let her down lightly and I can best do that by being very interested in somebody else. If I remain unattached, her little infatuation's going to get too big for her to handle, and she's sufficiently spoiled and headstrong enough to do something idiotic. You saw what she was like last night—and that's with no encouragement from me.'

Liz opened her mouth to give him a blistering reply, then closed it again swiftly. What on earth was the matter with her? Somewhere, beneath her dislike of being involved in other people's affairs, there was another emotion lurking, a sharp, spiky feeling that wanted to hurt—but she had only withdrawn from contact with her fellow men since Bev's death, never before had she wanted to give pain to anybody. She knew too much about pain to wilfully inflict it on somebody else, and Jean-Marc was quite right.

She recalled instances when she had been teaching— in a top-flight girl's' private school—when precocious sixteen-year-olds had made mincemeat of a male member of staff. She even remembered one young man who had left after only one term, a married man with a wife and children who had chosen unemployment rather than get involved with a little sexpot in the sixth form! Liz had giggled about it when she'd told Bev, but he hadn't laughed, he had been sorry for the man.

'Poor devil,' he had said. 'He didn't stand a chance. No man does against a really determined girl,' and then he had grinned. 'Look at me, I'm an example of a typical victim, shackled and bound to a determined woman. You caught me when I was too young to know how to fight back!'

'And how old would you have to be?' she recalled asking pertly, and Bev's laughing reply of, 'Ninety!'

She struggled back out of the past and into this present, to Jean-Marc watching her with his ruined face slightly smiling, not at her but at himself.

'I'm sorry,' she muttered almost grudgingly, 'I wasn't being very charitable, was I? I've been a teacher in a girls' school long enough to know better than to put all the blame on you.'

'You teach?'

'No, not now,' a shadow crossed her face. 'I gave it up about eighteen months ago to work at home as a translator.' The atmosphere between them seemed to have lightened, almost she was at ease, and she gave him a wry little grin. 'I taught French—but please, don't ask me to speak it! Eighteen months with no practice—I doubt I could even pass an A-level viva!' She made up her mind swiftly. 'Of course I'll come to the party. It's high time I indulged in a little French conversation, if only to keep my hand in. That's what you're doing, isn't it? Your English is very good.'

Jean-Marc nodded. 'It should be, I had ten years abroad; three in the States and seven in England, studying other farming methods and techniques and animal husbandry.'

'No wonder you're so good,' and the little squabble was forgotten as she listened to his descriptions of people and places—the intensely up-to-date pig farmer in Sussex who boasted of his hygienic sties and who had piped music played to his sows—the dour and monosyllabic sheepman in Northumbria who refused any modernisation on the grounds that his sheep would never take to new-fangled ways. And slowly Liz found herself feeling at ease, as though he was an old friend, not so old or friendly that she could talk to him about personal things, but a lot of her natural reserve vanished and she found herself laughing, something she hadn't done very much of since Bev had died.

The doctor came and went, rather disappointed that her injuries had been so slight; she thought the little man would have relished a case of severe concussion and was rather regretful she couldn't supply him with one, and at lunchtime, when the two boys returned, she joined them and Jean-Marc in the kitchen where she thoroughly enjoyed a very large herb omelette, served with large chunks of very fresh baguette, all the butter she could want and followed by a slice of apple tart which made her mouth water just to smell it.

After lunch, Ham and Louis got busy on the drive with Louis' metal detector and Ham, his red hair standing on end with excitement and his blue eyes shining in pleasant anticipation of discovering some long-abandoned treasure trove, waved aside her offer to help, so she went round to what she had thought was the back of the house; only it proved to be the front.

Here, the main door led down a flight of stone steps which split halfway down into two graceful curves that enclosed a miniature lake, and Liz was just hanging over the edge of it, trying to see if it contained any fish among the water-weed, when Jean-Marc came to join her.

'I thought all farmers lived very busy lives, no time for idleness,' she quipped. 'Or are you one of those gentleman farmer types, the ones who have a manager who does the real work while you sit back and rake in the profits?'

'Not at all,' he reproved. 'Since we have visitors, I'm giving myself this afternoon off, that's all. Tomorrow morning, I shall be hard at it as usual.'

Behind the dark lenses of her spectacles, she examined him, tall and slender but with a width to his shoulders which made her think of power. The bright sunlight glinted on his dark hair, smooth now, but she knew that if he rumpled it, it would fall into the same curls that bobbed on Louis' young head. And there was a faint air of French chic about him—his thin black trousers, creased to a knife edge, the sparkling whiteness of his fine linen open-necked shirt and the seemingly carelessly tied black silk cravat about his bronze throat. On holiday, Bev had always favoured baggy cords and tee-shirts and his rough fair hair had never been smooth.

Abruptly, Liz turned away from him to look once more into the water. It was no use to keep remembering Bev like this—he had gone, and no amount of wishing would ever bring him back. Marcie kept saying she should forget but forgetting was hard, especially when she had a cold loneliness which she could only fill by remembering. Over what seemed to be a great distance, she heard him repeat a question she must have missed.

'Tell me, Liz, do you like our house?' Perhaps it was

because he said 'house' and not 'home', or maybe the little prickle of caution which ran down her spine at his tone which warned her. She lifted her head from her rapt contemplation of the little ornamental lake and looked up at the imposing façade with its rows of long windows and the blue-slated, hipped roof.

'It's very imposing,' she answered colourlessly, and then because she felt some other comment was needed, 'The windows could do with a coat of paint, though. I suppose the summers, being so hot, play hell with paintwork.' Actually, she didn't like it. This garden was all right, the little lake, and behind that the sunken lawn with a sundial at the centre and a seat at the far end under some trees, but the house—no! Because that was what it was, a house, not a home. She had peeped into several rooms on her way down to lunch; a review of the *salon*, it was florid and reminded her of Versailles; the dining-room, striped paper, the clean dark lines of well polished mahogany in the Empire fashion, that too was a showcase and the little sitting-room, embroiderd tapestry chairs and firescreen; that too seemed to be more for display than for use.

Liz had almost expected to find a roped-off walkway and notices to visitors to keep to the route and not to stray into any of the apartments!

'Ah, you don't like it!' Jean-Marc sounded pleased, not hurt. 'Tomorrow morning, if you feel up to a kilometre walk, I'll show you something much better. At least, I hope you'll think it better.'

'What's that?'

'Wait till tomorrow,' he smiled his ruined smile. 'Be patient!'

The haul from the drive didn't contain her earring. Ham and Louis had unearthed a few centimes, a one-franc coin, a brass blazer button and a few small rusty nuts and nails, but they had been earnest and enjoyed themselves, so that they fell on dinner when it was served in the dining room. They wheeled in the meal on a huge trolley while Liz held her hands over her ears, expecting to hear the crash of breaking crockery, even flying to the rescue of a wobbling soup tureen which looked in danger.

After the meal, she was informed by Ham, he and Louis would wheel all the dishes back to the kitchen, and he was just in the middle of a graphic description of exactly how the trolley should be loaded when the telephone buzzed and Jean-Marc sent him out into the hall to answer it. Two minutes later he was back, redfaced and with shame in his blue eyes.

'Mum wants to speak to you, Liz,' and he caught at her dress as she went past him. 'I didn't mean to tell her, honestly. I tried not to, but she kept asking so many questions and I got muddled. It slipped out.'

'Forget it,' Liz rumpled his red head in passing, but she wasn't feeling as confident as she sounded. Unlike herself, Marcie was a small woman, but what she lacked in size, she made up in ferocity, and she also had an overwhelming mother complex.

'What's this Ham's been telling me?' Marcie's voice came over the wires full of a nebulous threat, and just for a second, Liz wished she need never set foot in England again, but her own voice, when she had an opportunity of answering, was calm and confident. In answer to an agonised, 'What have you done to my son?' she made light of the whole thing.

'I shook him up a bit, that's all. There's not a scratch on him, give you my word!'

'Ham said you drove straight into a tree!'

'So I did,' Liz tried to sound soothing, 'but Ham wasn't hurt. I was the only one with an injury.'

'You're not just saying that? Because if I thought you were—I'm supposed to go into hospital tomorrow—I wouldn't go, I'd be down there like a shot and I'd give you a piece of my mind!'

'He's unhurt!' Liz yelled into the mouthiece. 'I was the damaged one—I nearly split my head open—had to have a doctor. *Me!* Not your precious son!'

'Then that's all right.' Marcie heaved an audible sigh of relief and went off on another tack. 'A lovely-sounding man spoke to me last night, he said he was Louis' brother. What's he like?'

'Ten years old, small, dark and a pet,' Liz grinned fiendishly to herself as she admired a plaster nymph standing on a plinth against the wall.

'Not the boy,' Marcie scolded, 'the man, the one who rang to say you'd arrived. He sounded gorgeous and rather sexy. Is he married?'

'No,' Liz cooed back down the phone, 'and Dear Auntie Marcie, this is Worried Blue Eyes asking for advice. He carried me up to my bedroom, do you think he has evil designs on me? He's tall, dark and handsome, round about thirty-five or six, unmarried, and looks as though he's been around. Should I beware?'

'Grab him!' Marcie advised succinctly. 'He sounds just the job. I'll ring you tomorrow night from my bed of pain if I'm round from the anaesthetic. Ta-ta for now.'

'Don't hang up yet!' Liz nearly screamed. 'Don't you understand? I'm stuck here, marooned! My car's the next bext thing to a write-off, it'll take two weeks to repair it. . . .'

Her sister's reply was succinct and consisted of one word. *'Good!'* and she hung up, leaving Liz swearing at the dead black plastic in her hand.

She was decidedly flushed when she marched back into the dining-room and she took her seat with a thump while she glared at her nephew, who smiled at her unabashed. 'Is everything O.K. now?' he enquired meekly.

Liz straightened out her frown and thanked heaven for her dark glasses. 'Did you *have* to tell her?' she remonstrated gently.

Ham grinned. 'It slipped out with all the other things,' he explained. 'Crossing the Pont de Tancarville, going through that red light and being fined on the spot, losing our way outside Angers. I told her we'd had a smashing time so far.'

'Smashing's the right word,' Liz admitted. 'Ham, you're not a guardian angel after all, you're an evil genius. Avignon. . . .' she had been going to say that it seemed further away now than when they'd set off from Southampton, but Louis interrupted in a swift flood of French.

'You must stay here, Madame Liz. In Avignon, it will be very hot and uncomfortable, you will not like it. It is much more beautiful here and we have so many wonderful places to show you. Ham has made a list and I have found all the guide books. We have planned a little excursion for every day, and if Jean-Marc cannot take us, we will ride on the *autobus.* I like the *autobus,*' he added wistfully, 'and Berthe will give us food in a basket and we will have picnics. I like those as well.'

*'Tais-toi, mon brave!'* That was Jean-Marc being the elder brother, and there followed an exchange between the two, so fast that Liz's unaccustomed ear could

hardly pick out one word in twenty, but at the end of it, Loius was looking less strained.

'Did you understand, Liz?' and at her rueful headshake, Jean-Marc grinned. 'No? I didn't think you would. We slipped into the local patois, it comes more naturally to us. I told Louis that you would be staying for at least two weeks, that I would take you chateau visiting whenever I could and that, on Saturday evening, we would all go to Marie-France's birthday party.'

'I could wear my kilt for that.' Ham's eyes gleamed. He rather fancied himself in Highland dress and his kilt, sporran, long knitted socks and toy dirk to push into the top of one of them were all packed neatly at the bottom of his suitcase—which put Liz in mind of what she would wear herself, and in her mind she went over the contents of her own suitcase, not much of which was suitable as party wear.

French parties, she knew, tended to be prestigious affairs, everybody wearing their best—and her best was a tricel knit sheath in white which she'd crammed in at the last moment to cover dinners at hotels—a chain store dress, its only ornament a gold leather belt, but she had nothing else and she couldn't spare any of her supply of currency to buy anything better. It was as if Jean-Marc could read her thoughts.

'If you've nothing suitable to wear, I could drive you into Angers tomorrow and you could look in the shops,' he suggested, but she shook her head.

'I'm on a holiday, not on a buying spree,' she said firmly.

'But,' he pointed out with a pronounced twinkle in his eyes, 'look at the money you'll be saving by staying here. You'll be halving your hotel expenses. . . .'

'That's just the kind of remark which is guaranteeed to make me thoroughly bad-mannered,' she was swift in her reply. 'If you're going to mention things like that, I shall have no hesitation in offering to pay you for my keep!' She watched his brows lower into a straight-line frown and smiled serenely. 'The dress I have with me will do, it's not haute couture, not even a proper evening dress, but you won't be ashamed of me, I promise you.'

'Shame has little to do with it.' Jean-Marc's frown had vanished as quickly as it had come and his mouth curved into a smile. 'I should never be ashamed of you, Liz.'

There was a little warning voice in her head which was yelling 'danger, danger' and for a moment she was tempted to ignore it, but common sense won, that and the diversion caused when Ham and Louis, their peaches and yoghurt finished, started scrambling dishes together, intent on clearing the table as swiftly as possible.

'You trust them to do this?' Liz winced as plates clattered one on top of the other. 'You're very sanguine, I must say—that's all very lovely china.'

'They can break every piece,' he said it as if he hoped they would. 'Come along to the *salon*, Liz, while they clear the table, there's a fire lit there and the evening is getting chilly.' He turned to the boys. 'Half an hour, no more, after you've cleared the table and taken everything back to the kitchen,' he warned. 'Then Berthe will give you a hot drink before a bath and bed, so say "goodnight" now.' Liz noted their lack of argument and their docile departure with raised eyebrows.

'You *do* have the habit of command,' she said with

reluctant admiration, although she covered it well with a bitter-sweet sarcasm. 'You'll have to give me lessons in your technique—so far, I've had quite a struggle to get Ham to bed. I don't think his mother has all that much success either.'

'I've done my military service,' Jean-Marc said gravely, although the twinkle still lurked in his eyes. 'It made me impervious to beseeching looks,' and before she could move, he was round the table and there was a hand beneath her elbow. 'Come along to the fire, you'll be warmer. That's the trouble with these oversized rooms, you cook at one end and freeze at the other, and, as close as we are to the river, the evenings always feel damp.'

# CHAPTER THREE

IN the *salon*, Liz avoided the chaise-longue on which she had been laid the previous night, taking instead a wing armchair by the fireside. Jean-Marc approved her choice.

'It *is* hard and uncomfortable, isn't it? But unless the stuffing is very firm, the satin sags permanently, or so I was told. It's filled with horsehair,' he added, and then, 'Will you wait, I have to fetch the coffee.'

'Of course,' she answered him coolly as she arranged herself primly and composed her face into a polite expression of nothingness. 'I'm not at all sleepy.'

'Good.' He was already on his way out of the room. 'We'll have a talk when I return.'

'I'm looking forward to it.' It was a sweet, insincere answer but entirely lost on him; he was already out of the door and didn't hear it. Liz focused her attention on the oil paintings in their curly gold frames, mostly very dark portraits, but over the fireplace was a mammoth one of a battle, and she resolutely counted the cotton wool puffs of smoke coming from the cannon mouths. In the foreground Napoleon, on a skittish horse, was directing operations—there was no getting away from the man—and she recalled Bev's joke about him, that he must have been a neglected son who had developed a mammoth inferiority complex.

Jean-Marc came back in with the tray just as a sad little smile was curving her mouth. He put the tray down within easy reach, seated himself in a chair on the

42

other side of the fire—and his next words rubbed her on the raw.

'Your sister, Ham's mother, wasn't sympathetic?'

'No, she was not!' snapped Liz, and then relented. 'I suppose it's understandable, though. Ham's her son, I'm only her sister—and to be fair, although she thinks the world of him, she doesn't spoil him. With her husband away so much, she has to be both mother and father to Ham,' Liz chuckled softly. 'Which aggravates an already overbearing disposition,' she added. 'I shall probably never hear the last of this. Marcie's a splendid driver, she used to go rallying and she always said I didn't think fast enough. Now she *will* have something to crow about.' Hastily she changed the subject while she watched his swift, economical movement as he poured the coffee, almost fascinated by the way his long, slender hands moved so gracefully.

'Isn't it amazing how Ham and Louis communicate,' she said brightly, 'considering neither of them can speak the other's language.'

Jean-Marc gave her an understanding look, as though he knew she wanted to get off personal things. Obligingly, he climbed aboard her safe subject. 'They're neither of them completely ignorant of the other's language,' he pointed out mildly. 'Like any other boys, they don't care to sound foolish in front of adults, but between themselves, it doesn't matter. Ham has suggested Louis might come to his home for Christmas, did you know?'

Liz shook her head. 'Nobody tells me anything,' she said mock-mournfully. 'But he wouldn't have suggested it if my sister hadn't said it would be all right. I hope he does—that you allow him to come, I mean. Marcie has wonderful Christmases—Louis will enjoy himself.'

'And you, Liz, do you join in these wonderful Christmases?'

'I used to, but you know how it is—you leave home, have your own circle of friends. . . .' she finished lamely. Not for the world would she have told him that Marcie herself had made it impossible. Her sister's constant production of eligible men—Marcie's brisk attitude of 'it's time you forgot the past and made a new start'— the round of parties, where she was the odd man out, alone among all the merrymaking. 'I'm not really party material, I think. Which is why I'm feeling reluctant about this birthday do. Couldn't you possibly manage without me? I'd truly rather not go.'

'And rob me of your protection . . .?'

'Protection!' she snorted gently, and entered into the spirit of the game—for that was all it was a game. 'You, Jean-Marc, don't need anybody to protect you. What was it you said? Something about being able to manage with one hand tied behind your back?' Her eyes started to sparkle aggravatingly. 'Perhaps the best thing would be for you to stand back and watch Marie-France grow out of you.'

'She has this idea of marrying,' he murmured.

'So I heard,' Liz was no longer taking this very seriously. 'Lots of young girls do—marry older men, I mean. I think you should leave it to time, that's the best cure for what she's suffering from. One day, she'll notice your grey hairs. . . .'

'Ah!' he pretended to wince with pain. 'You've an abominable tongue when you give it free rein, Liz—I'm not that old, but I'm afraid. One day, Marie-France will take advantage of me, I'll be hustled up to the altar and stuck with a sexy nymphet for the rest of my life.'

'Which is probably no more than you deserve,' she answered hardily.

'*Vipère!*' His amused laughter roused her.

'Maybe,' she retorted with a smile. 'But surely that's better than being a coward—hiding from one woman behind the skirts of another. You should have been more alert, seen what was going on earlier.'

'But I didn't.' He tried to look innocent but somehow the expression didn't fit well on to the marred beauty of his face. Instead, he looked like a crestfallen satyr. 'The girl imagined everything, I assure you.'

'Or it could be *your* imagination,' Liz chuckled. 'A little wishful thinking. Pretend she doesn't mean it and perhaps she won't.'

'No, I daren't take the chance,' he told her mournfully, but his eyes were glinting with an outrageous mirth. 'So I must have you with me. You said you would come and I'm holding you to that.'

'I'll probably regret it,' she said sardonically. 'You've no intention of trying to flirt with me, I hope, because I warn you. . . .'

'The last thing to cross my mind,' he assured her.

Liz tucked herself into bed, warmed by a hot, milky drink and the two teaspoonsful of cognac which Jean-Marc had allowed her. She had passed an inactive day and she wanted to sleep, not lie awake thinking. Hospitality had been forced on her by circumstances beyond her control, and the best way was to accept it as gracefully as possible, not to make a big thing about it. And also to keep up this dryly humorous approach which she had just invented and which seemed to be working quite well. Once or twice when she had given Jean-Marc a tart answer, she had thought she had heard an echo of Marcie in her voice—which was no bad thing. The only time when she had really been herself was when he had suggested that, if her earring wasn't found, a jeweller he knew could possibly make one for her.

The thought of a substitute had wiped the smile from her face and she had rejected the offer, but at least she hadn't explained why. It just wasn't possible to explain to an almost complete stranger that the memory would be spoiled. That when she touched or looked at the bauble again, she would remember not Bev but Jean-Marc St Clair. Anyway, Ham seemed blissfully happy, which was a blessing, and just for a moment, Liz wished she was Ham's age and had his uncomplicated outlook on life—things would be so much easier.

'You be careful, my girl,' she muttered to herself in the darkness—and then decided the warning wasn't necessary. Jean-Marc wouldn't make things uncomfortable for her, not while she was staying in his house—at least, she hoped not. But men didn't seem to have much in the way of conscience—since she had been a widow she had learned not to accept an offer of friendship from a man—friendship was never what they had in mind! They seemed to think her lack of interest, her distaste and disinclination was her personal variation of a 'come-on'.

Times like this, she wanted desperately to talk to Bev. He had always been open and frank, he'd never had any dark corners which defied inspection. Whereas Jean-Marc was full of dark corners, he was the reverse of open. There, dammit, she was thinking of him again, wondering when he had developed those corners; he hadn't been born with them. Deliberately she turned her thoughts to her car. That was the important item;

without it. Avignon seemed too far away to reach. Her sister could be insulting and call it Liz's pilgrimage, but it was so much more than that. She, Liz was seeking a new beginning, and she had this idea that, if she ever found it, it would be in Avignon where she had been so happy. That was what she wanted to remember with love, not a green hillside and the grief which had followed.

In the morning, she woke to another beautiful day, and she dragged back the shutters to see dew sparkling on the tiny hedges which outlined the flower beds. It was still very early, but within the house, she could hear the sound of Ham and Louis going about their important affairs like finding swimming trunks and towels. There was the soft thud of their sneaker-covered feet as they descended the staircase and a couple of war whoops as they scampered along the flagged corridor to the kitchen.

Hastily she showered and dressed, hanging away the denim skirt and cotton shirt she had worn yesterday and sliding herself into jeans and a tee-shirt; arranging her hair to hide her temple and reluctantly adjusting the dark glasses on her nose. She wished she need not wear them, but the bruised cheekbone was now green with blue overtones and better hidden from view. When she arrived in the kitchen, Ham was solemnly sharing out small portions of the breakfast cereal he had brought with him. The box had suffered because he had packed several things on top of it, but the contents seemed to be in good shape. Liz smiled at his efforts and he became severe.

'There's really not enough to last,' he told her, and from that, she gathered she wasn't to ask for any.

'Why bother?' she grinned. 'When you're in Rome—

in this case France—you should as the French do, eat croissants.' She eyed the basketful on the table. 'There are some gorgeous ones here—this sort,' she indicated a long, bunlike shape, 'has a chocolate filling.'

'Louis likes my cereal and so do I,' Ham said flatteningly, 'and *of course* we're going to have croissants afterwards. We'd be jolly hungry if we didn't. If you see some of my cereal in a shop anywhere, you'll buy some for me, won't you?'

'Anything you ask.' Liz accepted a bowl of coffee from Berthe and entered into a one-sided conversation with the cook-housekeeper, who was eager to talk. Liz listened carefully; the *patois* was very thick and sounded quite unlike that which Jean-Marc and Louis had used. She cast a swift glance at the towering confection of starched lawn and lace that surmounted Berthe's nearly white hair and made an inspired guess. 'Brittany?'

*'Mais oui!'* Berthe appeared to think it was obvious to anybody, but she smiled and launched into another gabble. Liz listened intently, picking out a word here and there until at last she could get the sense of it. Jean-Marc had gone out early, but he would be back to take her out—a cardigan would be advisable, as the morning was still cool.

'You are getting your instructions.' That was Jean-Marc, looking all open-air in cords and a rough, thick shirt a well worn tweed jacket; moving silently despite his thick boots. 'Berthe is from the same village as my mother—she came here when I was born and she's been giving orders ever since.'

Liz let it pass and went on eating her croissants and drinking coffee stolidly while he chatted to the boys—sitting hitched on the corner of the old-fashioned dresser and smoking a cigarette while he disposed of two bowlsful of coffee.

'Time to go.' He stood up and offered a hand which she pretended not to notice. 'Are you ready, Liz? We won't wait for the boys, they'll catch us up on their bicycles.'

Ham and Louis passed them on the road, yelling that they would be back for lunch, before pedalling furiously on towards the small town of Villiers, and Liz gave a little sigh. 'Somehow,' she murmured, 'I get the idea I'm not wanted on this voyage.'

Jean-Marc gave a short, sardonic laugh. 'I told you,' he caught at her hand and gave it a comforting squeeze, 'you can't compare with the swimming instructor, especially one who gives out proficiency badges. But your turn will come—those badges will have to be sewn on their trunks. Women *do* have their uses!'

Liz sniffed and watched the boys as they speeded up to pass and repass each other. 'As long as they're safe,' she muttered.

'On this road,' he raised an eyebrow. 'It's very little used, most of the traffic takes the other road—there's only Villiers at the end of it, no other turn-off. They can't even got lost.'

'Sorry,' she made a face. 'I must sound like a mother hen, but my sister trusted me with him and a fine mess I've made of it so far. If anything happened to him, I don't think I'd dare go home!'

The road crossed a small stream and she would have liked to stop, but Jean-Marc hurried her on to turn into a cobbled yard surrounded by a huddle of well maintained farm buildings, and there he bade her wait while he went off into the farthest one, but of course she didn't. Her car was here somewhere, it was what she'd come to see, and she would find it.

Everything was silent except for animal noises, and the second door she pushed open looked promising. In the gloom, she could make out a dismembered tractor, and gradually, as her eyes became accustomed to the gloom, she saw the back of her car which presented a lovely, unscarred appearance. It wasn't so bad after all! And she walked round it to the front—where her momentary euphoria collapsed like a pricked balloon.

Mounted on a ramp, the Mini Traveller should have had its nose in the air, but there *was* no noise. There was something which bore a vague resemblance to an engine, some round things sticking out where Liz supposed the wheels fitted, and there was the starred, opaque windscreen—apart from that, nothing! It looked fit only for the breaker's yard.

'I told you to wait for me,' Jean-Marc's voice came from behind her. 'I said you shouldn't look at it.'

'Look at it?' Liz whirled round in a rage of despair. 'Why shouldn't I look at it—it's mine, isn't it? Aren't I to be allowed at the funeral? *you* look at it—that's what your damn tree did! It's only fit to be buried, so get it over with as soon as possible, will you? What's the good of anybody trying to tinker with *that*!'

'It's not as bad as it looks,' he put a comforting arm about her shoulders. 'New wings and a bonnet cover, a new grille and radiator, perhaps one new wheel and the windscreen replaced—there's nothing wrong with the engine and you haven't knocked anything out of line. . . .'

'And how long will all that take?' She was almost crying. 'Everything's spoiled—spoiled! I'll never get to Avignon!' It had been her lodestar for so long—once there, she would get everything straight, clear up the mess which was her life—be a member of the human race again instead of a cowering coward, unwilling to trust anybody, least of all herself.

'Do you think I wanted to come this way?' she raged. 'I didn't, I was doing a favour and just look where it's got me!' She wrenched herself free of his arm and slumped down on to the cold concrete floor, to wrench off her sunglasses and bury her face in her hands while scalding tears ran down her face.

Jean-Marc dropped down beside her and drew her close. 'It's nowhere near as bad as it looks,' he soothed. 'A couple of weeks and it'll look like new. Liz!' he gave her a little shake, 'there are worse things in life than a broken car.'

'Two weeks—you keep on about two weeks!' She refused to be mollified as she raised her wet face and looked at him with dislike. 'And I should be grateful for that? There won't be enough time left to do what I wanted to do, go where I wanted to go; I needed at least three. . . .'

'. . . . You need a cup of coffee,' he interrupted unfeelingly. 'Come,' and he hauled her to her feet and half led, half dragged her out into the sunlight of the cobbled yard.

Moodily, Liz went with him, but stopped short when, after crossing the yard, he led her through a gate in a high wall, along a path and paused at what looked like the porch of a private house. She didn't want to meet anybody, not at this moment, and she dragged herself back from him. Hadn't he any sense, trying to make her meet people when she was upset, her nose pink and her eyelids puffy with weeping?

'It's all right,' it was as though he could read her thoughts, 'there's nobody here. This is what I was telling you about yesterday—it's the original farmhouse, quite empty. It's being done up. But here, we can make ourselves some coffee—the electrician finished the rewiring yesterday, and of course there's a bit of a mess.'

Liz stood in the hallway amid the smells of wood shavings, putty and paint, all the strange, clean smells of a new house, but as he had said, this wasn't new. Her eyes caught the gleam of a polished old banister rail ending in a sturdy, carved newel post and the worn treads of the curving staircase. 'What is this place?' she asked.

He pushed open a door and she followed him into a sunlit kitchen where shining new units ranged around the freshly painted walls and a new electric cooker glinted with chrome and white enamel.

'Dieudonné.' Jean-Marc was finding things with economical movements. A coffee filter machine, a tin of coffee, sugar, a couple of buttercup yellow mugs; he rattled in a drawer for teaspoons and filled the reservoir of the machine from the tap over the sink. 'The original Dieudonné.'

Liz turned her back to look out of the window over the neatly tilled garden while she surreptitiously wiped at her eyes and replaced her spectacles, almost taking cover behind the smoked lenses. 'Very nice,' she muttered sullenly. 'What's it for?'

'It's to be my home, mine and Louis'.' He kept it simple. 'This is where I was born, where I lived for the first eighteen years of my life and where I intend to live for the rest of my life.'

Liz walked across the newly tiled floor and looked out of the window. 'It feels a nice place,' she murmured almost to herself. 'It's warm and friendly but if this is Dieudonné, what's that place?' and she gestured at a distant clump of trees, where the blue slate, hipped roof of the house they had just left glimmered through the leafy branches. Jean-Marc followed her across to the window when he had switched on the coffee maker.

'That,' he said in a derisory tone, 'that is a monster, a house with an insatiable appetite for money.' Liz glanced up at him from under her lashes to see his face a mask of dislike. 'This is my home and I intend to live here, close to my work and my animals and to everything I knew when I was a boy and a young man. It's where I belong and where Louis belongs. He also is my father's son. Neither of us belongs in that mockery of a home up the road with its painted ceilings, the paintings bought by the half dozen and the fake antique furniture.'

He directed her attention to the meadow beyond the small orchard at the bottom of the garden where, ankle-deep in the grass, cows were grazing, their red and white coats glossy with wellbeing.

'Normandy cattle.' He looked at them contentedly. 'Descendants of those my mother brought here as part of her *dot*. She was a farmer's daughter and she used to help milk them herself until my father installed the milking machines.'

'Then how did you come to leave here, go to live in that other house, if you liked this one so much better? Surely. . . .'

'Life happened.' Jean-Marc both sounded and looked enigmatic, and Liz suddenly understood—this was part of his disillusion—not all of it, something far worse had happened to him to give him those tortured eyes. She stayed silent and waited; he would either tell her or brush it aside, and she rather hoped he would tell.

'My mother died when I was sixteen,' he told her

sombrely, 'and my father and I lived alone for two years. It wasn't so comfortable, but we had Berthe to care for us, we had the farm and a small vineyard and there was always plenty to do. At eighteen, I went off to do my national service for two years and I didn't come home as often as I should have done—in fact, when I'd finished my two years, I went to the Legion for another two. I was having my first taste of freedom, and I think it went to my head a little.'

'It usually does,' Liz grimaced as she remembered her own mother's scoldings when she had first gone to college. The 'Darling, we miss you—we never seem to see you nowadays—you don't ever seem to have time to come home'. Liz had regretted that carelessness later on when her parents had both died within three months of each other and only she and Marcie were left.

'Did it for you as well?' Jean-Marc looked at her understandingly.

'Mmm,' she nodded. 'I was sorry afterwards—they both died, you see.'

'So was I, although my father didn't die.' Jean-Marc smiled, but there was no humour in it, only a dreadful sad mockery. 'My father remarried, a young *assistante* at the *école des enfants* in Villiers,' he became reminiscent. 'She was here before I went away; young, very beautiful—all the young men were after her, me included—but when I came home, it was to find she'd married my father. It was she who wanted that house,' he nodded to the blue roof through the trees. 'My father bought it for her and this place was turned into flats for summer visitors. He took the name "Dieu-donné" with him and this became just La Ferme de Dieudonné.'

'And yet, liking the house, wanting it, your

stepmother now prefers to live in Paris?' Liz allowed a slight query to colour her words. To her, it didn't make sense.

He shrugged as he set out the mugs, took a jug of milk from the fridge and rooted in a cupboard for a bottle of cognac. 'Perhaps she became bored with it,' and he closed his mouth firmly as he poured the coffee, then his face broke into a smile as he waggled the cognac bottle before her eyes. 'It's good for shock—I'll put a little in your cup. It'll be about another five or six weeks before we can move back here. Tell me, do you think Berthe will like her new kitchen?'

Liz was now more composed and she tried to fill her mind with the kitchen, but she wasn't completely successful; the Mini Traveller would keep obtruding, but she tried not to let it show. 'She ought,' she growled. 'It's very well thought out and these non-slip cork floor tiles are wonderful.' As she was speaking, the Mini receded from her mind—perhaps it wasn't so bad after all—maybe it *could* be repaired; she began to take an interest. After all, she was Jean-Marc's guest, no matter how unwillingly. He was doing his best to entertain her, in his way—it would be churlish to keep harping on her woes.

'When we've had coffee and I've got over my attack of the miseries, may I see the rest of the house?' and just for a second she saw him nearly as he must have been when he was young and carefree, his eyes no longer hooded and the disillusion gone from his smile.

'With pleasure, Liz. I was only waiting to be asked.'

The coffee was hot and fragrant and she buried her nose gratefully in the deep mug while, for the first time in three years, she allowed herself to think about somebody else rather than her own grief. This man, she suspected he might be jealous of his stepmother—he certainly seemed very attached to his own mother, or—she speculated on—could he have been jealous of his father? He'd said he'd been after the girl himself. It must have been an almighty shock to come home and find his erstwhile girl-friend married to his own father!

She wrinkled her nose involuntarily—there was something unpleasant about that last thought. Liz cleared it from her mind, or tried to, but it stayed there in her subconscious, a grey little trail of distaste, giving rise to all sorts of speculation, some so horrifying that she clamped down on her thinking and broke the companionable silence.

'Is this all that's ready—in the house, I mean, or has everything else been made bright and shiny?'

'Very little is new.' Jean-Marc offered more coffee, but she shook her head. 'I'm using most of the original furniture, it's all been stored in the big barn, under tarpaulins, but it hasn't come to much harm.' He glanced around him with an air of content. 'This place is far older than the house we occupy at present. A gift, I believe, to a man who was willing to marry a 'little friend' of a long-dead de Villiers. That was the aristocratic family in this area and things like that often happened—the child would then be born with an inheritance provided and all the trappings of respectability.'

Liz chuckled as she saw the funny side. 'And they called this "Dieudonné?" That means "gift of God".'

Jean-Marc's smile was wide and uncomplicated. 'In those days, before the Revolution, that's what the de Villiers thought themselves to be—gods!' He took the empty coffee mugs and swilled them out before putting them on the drainer. 'Do you feel a little happier now, Liz?'

'Mmm.' She walked beside him and peeped into what she thought must be the salon; low-ceilinged and the walls half panelled and with fire-dogs set in a yawning grate before they went up the curve of the staircase. 'I'm not really unhappy and I'm sorry I made such a fuss, but,' she paused on a stair, 'I think it's quite understandable, in the circumstances. My plans. . . .'

'Those plans!' Jean-Marc shook his head at her and put a hand under her elbow, urging her to the top of the flight, where they stood on a broad gallery which ran the length of the house. 'This,' he pushed open a door, 'is the master bedroom; my parents used to occupy it. I had the carpenter start on this straight away. I can manage without the *salon* or any of the other downstairs rooms all I need is the kitchen and somewhere to sleep. As you can see, it's finished, and we start on the rooms for Louis and Berthe tomorrow.'

Liz walked past him into the room; it was a good size and simply furnished with only the necessities. The bed dominated, which she supposed was as it should be, and there were no knick-knacks, no pots and bottles on the polished top of the dressing-table, no signs of human possession—that would come later when the room had an occupant. The ceiling over the window followed the slope of the eaves, falling so low where it met the wall, she need hardly reach up to touch it, and she pulled back one shutter to fill the room with sunlight.

'Yes,' she sniffed appreciatively at the smell of polish and new paint. 'It's homey. My parents had a room like this—sort of family, not fashion.'

Jean-Marc was behind her as she looked out of the window—she didn't need to turn to see him, she could feel him, the warmth of his body, the faint aroma of cologne and tobacco—he was near, but she couldn't move, not even when she felt his hands on her shoulders, pulling her back to rest against him. He was hardly touching her, yet she felt her breasts swell and harden, straining against the stuff of her tee-shirt, and she nearly wept for this weakness which she suddenly couldn't control.

An ice-cold part of her explained silently: 'It's been a long time, too long; but that wasn't good enough and she knew it. During the last two years, there had been many opportunities, many offers from men willing to console her for her loss, but she had had no hesitation in refusing them all. The hesitant, the brash, she'd sent them all on their way with a flea in their ear—the hesitant because they had permanent ideas and she couldn't and wouldn't think about permanency with anybody but Bev—and the brash, the ones who said she should have a little fun—dear heaven, they had the gall to call it 'fun'!—they had been dismissed because they cheapened and dirtied what she had felt for her husband. To them, 'love' was a steamy night in bed, no tenderness or commitment.

She could feel herself start to tremble, and when Jean-Marc's mouth came warm in the curve of her neck, she gave a little thoaty moan, not of fear or pleasure but something in between. She felt his hands slide under her tee-shirt and up, to close on her breasts, and she strained away from him automatically while her heart wept.

'No!' she muttered, trying to twist away from him, and then, smoothly and without effort, he turned her to face him.

'No?' He kept one arm about her and tilted her face with a long finger under her chin; she saw his smile and felt the dark glasses plucked from her nose. There were little flickering yellow flames behind the grey of his eyes, flames which promised all the things she had lost three years ago. Warmth, passion, love; they were all there in his eyes, in the warm pressure of his body against hers. Silly thoughts ripped through her mind—body language, this man knew all about that, he could do this without a word, he knew where to touch and, when his mouth found hers, how to kiss—and then she was standing alone and he was at arm's length and looking at her with all the old mockery.

'I wasn't going to force myself on you, Liz. There was no need for you to go as stiff as a board.

'Force yourself on me?' Her laugh was too loud and a bit hysterical. 'What a silly idea! I mean, what could you do—I've a mind of my own. . . .'

'Exactly.' Grey eyes glittered down at her; eyes which said they knew just what was the matter. She looked again and her heart gave an extra beat. Those eyes knew everything, there was a world of knowledge in their depths, and to save herself, to hang on to the cool 'woman of the world' image which she had cultivated for so long. . . .

'Please, don't spoil it,' she used the first thing that came to mind, 'I'm still a bit off balance—the crash—everything—I've got this feeling you're rushing things. . . .'

'How long do you need?' Jean-Marc raised an arched eyebrow and his mouth curved into an understanding smile. It was the smile that did it! Suddenly, Liz was no longer afraid, the tingling left her body and she was ice-cold, filled only with defiance. So apparently he was used to easy conquests and he'd thought she'd be one, even though she had already given him a warning. In that case, he had to be taught a lesson—he would learn, as several other men had learned, but this time she wouldn't be brusque and get it over quickly—this time she'd be cruel. She wouldn't nip it in the bud, as she had done so often before. Jean-Marc St Clair should learn the hard way. Words bubbled up on to her tongue and trickled off easily.

'About a couple of weeks,' she murmured. 'In fact,' she continued, a trace of flirtation in her voice, 'I can safely say that by the time my car's ready to take the road, I shall be in a state where I can cope with almost anything.' She looked up at him with wide, innocent blue eyes. 'Now may I have my sunglasses back, please? I feel naked without them, and if you've the time to spare, might I see a little more of your farm? I'm particularly fond of animals, especially young ones. . . .'

'We have a few piglets,' he offered, and there was relctant admiration on his face.

'Lovely,' she cooed back at him—she was overdoing it a bit, but that was better than standing dumbly and waiting for him to take the initiative. 'I've always liked piglets, little pink things with such ridiculous, dainty little feet. They're so pretty,' and with a great deal of self-possession, she walked past him, out of the room and down the stairs.

# CHAPTER FOUR

'BUT you promised!' Ham, red hair bristling and his blue eyes bright with indignation, surveyed his aunt angrily in the mirror, and Liz laid down her palette of eye-shadow while she attempted to reason with him.

'I don't think I mentioned any specific time, Ham. I said I'd hang on until my car was ready—I could hardly do anything else. Now, it's almost finished, so I *must* go on, you know that.'

'But Mum said I had to. . . .' and Ham stopped, his face almost as red as his hair.

'Your mum said. . . .?' Liz raised an eyebrow. She tried hard to remember that Ham was only twelve, that Louis was an interested spectator in all this and that icy remarks and bad language were out! 'Perhaps it would be better if you told me exactly what your mum said,' she suggested mildly. 'It might help to get things straight in my mind.'

'On the phone,' Ham muttered fiercely. 'She said she didn't want you to go Avignon—she told Jean-Marc as well—she said we had to keep you here for as long as possible—she said she didn't care if the car was never repaired and we had to go home by train, so we tried to make things as nice as possible, Louis and me.'

'But that's interference with the liberty of the individual,' Liz pointed out gently.

'But you've had a good time, haven't you?' Ham insisted. 'Louis and me, we've worked hard planning things, and you said you enjoyed seeing those chateaux, and we've made out a programme for next week as well. Louis had a splendid idea for one day. . . .'

'And what's that?' Liz turned back to the mirror and recommenced work on her eyes. This was the night of Marie-France's birthday party and she wanted to look good—all trace of bruising had vanished from her cheekbone, so she could no longer hide behind her sunglasses and, she told herself, her desire to look her best was a perfectly natural thing; any woman going to a party would feel the same.

'Louis says that Jean-Marc will take us all down the river to St Nazaire, if we ask him. Louis says it's a smashing boat and quite big. They use it for fishing and for carrying heavy things to and from Nantes. There's an engine as well as a sail so it can come up the river pretty quickly. . . .'

'It would make a change from chateaux visiting,' Liz said dryly. 'That is beginning to be a pain in the neck— no, I mean it—staring up at battlements, up at ceilings and up at portraits, I actually *do* get a pain. Very well, just a couple more days, but only if my car isn't ready. . . .'

'You do not like to see chateaux?' Louis piped up from the background, and she eyed him suspiciously. Over the last four days, she had begun to suspect he knew a lot more English than he had admitted to—that he'd been pulling the wool, not only over her eyes but over Jean-Marc's as well, but she had never been able to collect any cast-iron evidence to support her theory. If she was right—she scowled and her hand slipped so that blue eye-shadow went on a bit too thickly—was that another ploy they'd thought up to keep her stranded in the Loire valley? She decided to take a chance on Ham's noted ability to put his foot in it.

'Why, Louis,' she gushed while she brushed away the blue so that her eyes matched, 'you speak quite good English!'

Ham didn't disappoint her. ' 'Course he does,' he broke in, then went red again. 'But you won't tell, will you, Liz?' he pleaded. 'Louis says it's like having a trump card nobody knows about. He says it might be useful if he ever has to r. . . . What I mean is. . . .' He and Louis looked at each other and the younger boy shrugged fatalistically before he gave a reluctant nod. 'Louis has reasons, Liz, honestly! He wouldn't run away just for the fun of it. I mean, he's told me a lot you don't know about.'

'Then don't tell me any more,' Liz sighed, wielded a lipstick and blotted her mouth. 'I don't think I'd better know.' She dragged her kimono about her and turned from the mirror. 'Off you go, both of you. I'm going to dress; and while I'm about it, you both look very smart.'

Louis gave her a sideways, glinting smile. 'Ham is beautiful,' he said mischievously.

'You're both beautiful—go on now, shoo!' Liz grinned as they scampered out. Louis in long black trousers, small patent leather black shoes and with a neat black velvet bow at the collar of his white shirt, and Ham—Liz smiled fondly. Ham always looked as though he was growing out of his ordinary everyday clothes, but tonight, in his precious kilt and sporran, ruffled shirt, black velvet jacket and long Argyll-patterned knitted socks, he looked exactly right. The socks disguised his thin legs, the kilt hid his bony knees and his scrawny wrists were concealed by the lace-trimmed ruffles on his shirt-sleeves.

As for herself, she wrinkled her nose at the day-length white tricel knit dress. She had intended it for evenings in hotels, but it didn't look too bad really—perfectly plain, round-necked and sleeveless—she would be all right as long as she didn't stand next to a Dior creation. She slipped a thin gold chain about her neck, hung large gold Creole hoops in her ears and stood well back to get the overall picture. Her legs looked fine, her high-heeled white strappy sandals had cleaned up nicely and she was a good shape underneath the plain dress. Had she been a bit heavy-handed with the eye make-up? It was a long time since she'd used this much, but no, she didn't think so, and her newly washed hair, bleached by a few days in the sun, hung in a swinging silver bell to her shoulders.

With a sigh of regret at having to spoil the picture, she picked up her green nylon anorak and went downstairs to where Jean-Marc was waiting for her in the *salon*. The temperature between the two of them had been cool since the episode at the farmhouse, at least on Liz's side, and although he had driven them on their vists to Chinon, Saumur and Ussé; she, Ham and Louis had visited Montreuil Bellay by bus; Liz had concentrated exclusively on the two boys. She had congratulated herself that her manner was precise and had exactly the right attitude, one of cool remoteness—not unfriendly but remote; also that she had put Jean-Marc St Clair firmly in his place.

The trouble with the man was that he flatly refused to stay in the place she had put him; he insisted on being friendly, humorous and in indulging in a mere hint of flirtation. Nothing she could put her finger on, but it was there, in his eyes and in the curve of his sensuous mouth. Like now, when he twitched the anorak from her hand and laid a shawl of white wool about her shoulders.

'No,' as her hand went to remove it, 'let it stay, it's a gift from Berthe, and you wouldn't wish to hurt her feelings, would you?'

'It's very kind of her,' Liz muttered—why, oh, why did she have to be so conscious that they were alone together in this room, why did she have this little prickle of frightened excitement running down her spine? There was nothing to be frightened of and no cause for excitement that she could see. 'I couldn't possibly take such a beautiful thing,' she muttered as she admired the silk floss that made the deep fringing.

'Why not?' He raised an eyebrow. 'Berthe makes things like this in her spare time, she has a drawer full of them. If you refuse it, she'll be hurt. Would you like a drink before we leave, there's a bottle of Vouvray I'd like you to try.'

'No, thanks,' she said definitely; tonight, she thought, was going to be one time when she would need all her wits about her. There didn't seem to be anything for her to say, so she seated herself on the uncomfortable chaise-longue, aware all the time that it wasn't only the hard seat which was causing her discomfort. This was a purely mental thing, something in the atmosphere which was stifling thought and making her mind numb. She wanted to say something, anything to relieve the rapidly growing tension, but words wouldn't come, her mouth was too dry to say them anyway, and unconsciously she licked her lips and wished Ham and Louis would hurry up. The words broke from her involuntarily and fell from her stiff lips in a hardly intelligible mutter.

'What's keeping Ham and Louis? They were ready when I saw them nearly twenty minutes ago.'

'A small matter of tidiness.' Jean-March was

unperturbed. 'I looked into their bathroom and bedroom before I came downstairs and I sent them back to clear up the mess they'd left.'

'All boys are untidy,' Liz parroted her sister. 'Why didn't you call me, I'd have put it right.'

'All boys are *not* untidy,' he retorted vehemently. 'Or if they are, it's because some woman has spoiled them rotten. Louis knows better than to leave the bathroom in that condition—soiled clothes and wet towels all over the floor and the soap melting in a pool of water. There's no woman to run round after them here, clearing up their mess. . . .'

'And I suppose you're blaming it all on Ham?' The feeling of oppresion had gone from the room as if a high wind had blown through and removed it—Liz became animated. 'Perhaps,' she suggested silkily, 'it would be better if, as soon as my car's ready, I take him with me. I'm sure his mother wouldn't like to think Louis was picking up bad habits.'

'Don't be a fool, Liz,' he snorted. 'There's no need for you to stand on your dignity because I've reprimanded the boys; neither need you put all the blame on Ham. Louis doesn't need to be led astray, he has his full quota of bad habits which I'm trying to cure, with varying degrees of success.'

'Something to do with your army training, I suppose,' she was sweetly vindictive. 'What were you, a sergeant-major?'

'No-o!' Jean-Marc was laughing at her. There wasn't a smile on his face, but she could feel waves of merriment washing over her and for a moment she almost smiled. Almost but not quite; just in time, she remembered the danger. Give this man an inch and he'd not be content with a mile, he'd want to go the whole distance. He was making his bid for that inch now.

'There's not much difference between a boy and a girl, not at Ham and Louis' age,' he continued smoothly. 'So why would you expect a girl to be neat, clean and tidy while a boy is allowed to get away with murder? They made a mess—there's nobody to clear it up except one overworked, middle-aged cleaning woman—so they must do it themselves. That way, they'll learn not to makes messes.'

It was only what she had said so often to Marcie, but Marcie had never been the receptive type and her reply was always the same. 'Don't make such a fuss about a little thing, Liz—it won't take me a few seconds to clear it up. Boys will be boys, you know.' Liz stiffened her spine and glared at Jean-Marc. Over the past three days, she had come to one inescapable conclusion. There must not be one point of real contact between her and this man or she might be destroyed completely. She had survived her three years of widowhood by isolating herself, living on memories—one of those memories was of Bev leaving the bathroom in an unholy state of disorder—and in that isolation, she'd been safe; subjugating her natural desires with no difficulty at all.

She had never fancied any of the men who had appeared only too willing to take Bev's place—how could she, when the memory of him was so sharp and clear, but Jean-Marc was different. Him she could fancy if she let herself—but she wasn't going to. For him, it would be a holiday romance, a brief, hot thing to be forgotten as easily as it started, an insult to her memory of Bev and a cheap thing which she would never be able to live with.

'It's something on which we'll just have to differ,' she

said icily. 'Ham and Louis are on holiday, so I don't see why they shouldn't have a little freedom from rules and regulations. Ham's never had to put up with those anyway, my sister is an understanding mother.' She strove to keep the squabble going. 'She's firm, but only about important things. I realise your difficulty, of course, and I'll have a word with Ham, but I think the most sensible thing would be to take him with me when I leave for Avignon.'

'Don't be a fool, Liz!' Jean-Marc was appearing to lose his temper, his nostrils had thinned and his mouth was a straight line of displeasure. 'You're making a mountain out of a molehill and doing it deliberately for some reason of your own.'

'Nothing of the kind,' she snapped back at him. 'I just don't care to leave my nephew where I feel he might not be happy.'

'Then why not ask him?' The spurt of temper had died away and his face was its usual wearily mocking mask. 'I can hear them coming now, so here's your opportunity, give the boy a free choice.' The mockery increased. 'I know what his answer will be if you don't.'

And that was just the trouble, Liz did know. Ham would fight tooth and nail to stay here with Louis—he would accept Jean-Marc's discipline without question, he liked the man, whereas she was a rather peculiar aunt, a bit addled in the head.

'Don't you?' he repeated the question, and she found herself smiling ruefully.

'Mmm,' she admitted generously. 'Wild horses wouldn't drag him away with me, he's having too good a time, and after the impact he's going to make tonight in his Highland gear. . . .'

'Exactly.' Jean-Marc gave her a warm, heartbreaking

smile and she cursed herself for being so easily brought round.

The scolding had had little or not effect on either Ham or Louis, they erupted into the room with no appearance of having been cowed. Louis was smiling sweetly and Ham had lost none of his usual ebullience. Liz was beginning to be suspicious of that smile of Louis', she was starting to believe it covered a sharp little brain, not only sharp but deadly determined but when he addressed her in French, she went along with it and didn't give him away. At least she was one up on Jean-Marc; she knew something he didn't—or did she? She flicked him a glance from under her lashes, but his face was, as usual, unreadable.

'We'll be late,' Ham scolded her. 'I thought you'd be all ready to go—probably out in the car waiting for us.'

To cover an awkward moment, Liz seized his ear and muttered the time-honoured question, 'I hope you're wearing pants under that skirt!'

Ham grinned at her, he'd heard it too frequently for it to upset him. ' 'Course I am, silly! Although,' his blue eyes sparkled with mischief, 'they're not really necessary, you know. Louis wants one like it—do you think, if he comes at Christmas . . .?'

'Sure of it!' she replied in a stage whisper. 'Leave it to your mum.'

Liz gave a silent groan of despair as they approached the door of the hotel dining-room. Through it she could see the great horseshoe of tables spread with snowy cloths, there was the sparkle of glassware and cutlery, the hum of conversation and just inside the door, the doctor and Marie-France waited to receive their guests. Any hopes she might have cherished that she would be able to slide in unnoticed died the death; the party from

Dieudonné was among the last arrivals and everybody's eyes were on them.

'You fixed this, didn't you?' she hissed at Jean-Marc under cover of giving him a grateful smile. 'Messy bathroom indeed! It was just a delaying tactic!' And she felt her hand grabbed by the little fat doctor and watched as he kissed her knuckles, but surreptitiously she was examining Marie-France, tonight playing the *jeune fille* in white organza with a jade green sash.

The doctor passed her on to his daughter, who greeted her charmingly except for the nasty glint in her green eyes, but somehow that glint steadied Liz so that she could press her prettily wrapped packet containing an emerald green chiffon scarf into the girl's hand and express the hope that she would have many more wonderful birthdays, and then she was in the clear while Jean-Marc had both his cheeks kissed by the doctor and fell into Marie-France's clutches. Out of the corner of her eye, Liz watched him extricate himself, admiring his elderly uncle attitude, and then his hand was under her elbow as he steered her towards the tables.

'A small mistake,' he murmured in her ear as he picked up the little card bearing Louis' name and went swiftly down to where Ham and his brother were deep in dispute. 'Thank you, *mon p'tit*.' He took a card from Louis' hand and came back to put it against the place setting next to his own. 'Louis will be more happy to sit with Ham, don't you think?'

'I wonder you ever get invited anywhere,' Liz couldn't resist a smile. 'Mucking around with other people's arrangements! I've never seen this before in France, though, I thought it was only the English and Americans who went in for this regimentation.'

'Oh, we're just as regimented,' his eyes twinkled,

'although not usually at a party like this where aunts, uncles and cousins automatically take their place in strict order of seniority.'

'Which would have put you well down among the mere acquaintances.' Her eyes sparkled and he gave her a lopsided smile.

'I said I'd need protection,' he pointed out, 'and I don't care to have my hand forced, not by a little white card. Did you go to many parties while you were in France?' He chuckled at her look of surprise. 'Yes, Liz, I know the pattern. If you taught French, you had to be qualified to do it, and that means you spent a year here at one of our schools as an *assistante*. Where was it?'

'The Lycée Daniel Fortin in Bourges,' she admitted. 'I lodged with two dear old ladies and developed an accent which labelled me as a "*berichonne*", but that was more than five years ago, before I was married, and times change. My two old ladies were very formal, very correct; they were sisters, yet I never heard them call each other anything but Madame Delon and Madame Carpentier.'

'It's not unusual among the older generation.' The doctor and Marie-France had come to the head of the table and Jean-Marc gave Liz a gentle push into her chair. 'Old habits die hard, especially in rural areas where the population is small. You see all those birthday gifts?' he nodded to a table by the door which was loaded with packages. 'They'll mostly contain linen—all in readiness for—er. . . .' he hesitated, and Liz supplied the phrase he wanted, hoping he would understand it.

'Mademoiselle Debret's bottom drawer?' and at his nod, 'How very unexciting! I know what I'd have said if somebody had given me a pair of pillowcases for my seventeenth birthday!' Talking to Jean-Marc like this was easy and she hoped she would be able to keep it up for the rest of the evening. It was relaxing as well, no undercurrents, and had it not been for the venomous glow in Marie-France's eyes whenever they lighted on her, Liz would have enjoyed herself. She ate very little of the gorgeous food and made one glass of wine last all through the meal, and afterwards when everybody went into the ballroom, a one-storied addition to the hotel which overlooked the gardens at the back of the building, Jean-Marc stuck firmly to her side despite all efforts to dislodge him.

'You don't have to stick to me like glue,' she protested, 'your *mademoiselle* is dancing with her father, you're quite safe.'

'Only until the music stops,' he murmured. 'After that, she chooses her own partner—so,' he slid a hand beneath her elbow, drawing her to her feet, 'we'll make sure it isn't me. Do you think you could look as though you're enjoying yourself? You're wearing a martyred look.'

'You'll be doing that before long.' Liz painted a tight smile on her lips as she slipped into his arm. 'I haven't danced for years, I'm out of practice, so, if you value your toes,' she pulled away from him slightly, 'you'll keep your feet where I can't tread on them.'

'Relax,' he admonished as she stiffened against him, and she bit her lip with effort. Relax was one thing she daren't do, instead she fixed her eyes on the perfection of the knot of his bow tie and concentrated fiercely on building up her morale. Beneath her fingers, where they rested lightly on his shoulder, she could feel, through the layers of cloth, the bulk of bone and muscle—the movement of their two bodies so close together was a torture to her, it invoked a lot of feelings which she could very well do without, and the lack of words between them only heightened the effect until it was all she could do not to break away from him and run screaming from the room. And that was something else he knew, damn him! The only thing was to start up a little conversation; thinking up something to say, paying attention to his answers and thinking up some more ought to take her mind off this abominable closeness.

'I suppose I ought to use the remainder of my short stay in practising my oral French,' she made it light and brittle. 'It's amazing how only dealing with the printed word makes one dumb. Always having a dictionary at hand makes one lazy—one doesn't bother to remember....'

'Try it out on me,' he advised. 'If you can't think of anything to say offhand, repeat after me, 'Jean-Marc, thank you for bringing me to this ghastly party....'

'No! I won't thank you for that,' she interrupted fiercely. 'I didn't want to come, remember? Nobody wants me here, least of all the birthday girl, and so far you've managed to give an impression of the man in possession, fiddling place names and—and everything. It might suit you very well as a kind of smoke screen, but it doesn't suit me. I don't like deception. Oh lord, what have we done now, everybody's looking at us!'

'The music's stopped,' he was aggravatingly calm, 'and we've been so immersed in each other that we didn't notice....'

'... and Mademoiselle Debret is heading this way with the light of battle in her eyes. I think I shall surrender you to her tender mercies.'

'Which will leave you stuck with the doctor,' he smiled down at her aggravatingly, 'and I can't allow that. He's getting on in years and you'd be bad for his blood pressure. We'll go outside to cool off.'

Liz looked out through the wide windows at a smooth, grassy area which sloped down to a small river—the same river, a tiny tributary of the Loire which she had crossed on her way from Dieudonné to the farm; at shrubs, trees and flowers all silvered by moonlight, and shuddered away from the prospect of being alone out there with Jean-Marc. He was too damned attractive, too experienced.

'No, thank you,' she answered sedately. 'You have a duty dance, so why not get it over as soon as possible? As for the doctor, I'll spare his blood pressure and join Ham and Louis. They look as though they're enjoying themselves,' and with a fixed, sweet smile, she walked serenely down the length of the ballroom to where the boys were capering in a grotesque imitation of their elders.

Ham provided her with a can of Coke, detached himself from a frilly little girl of about eight who was clinging to him and grinned at her in his open, uncomplicated way. 'This is smashing, isn't it—or it would be if it wasn't for the kids.' The frilly child had crept up on him again and he twitched his kilt away from her fingers. 'I'm having a jolly good time.'

'And Louis?' The French boy was no longer capering, he had seated himself on one of the spindly-legged gilt chairs and was staring out at the dancers and for a moment he looked very much like the grown-up Jean-Marc, his small, angelic face expressing disillusion. Ham glanced at his friend.

'Oh, he'll be all right, it's just her!' he nodded his red head to where Jean-Marc and Marie-France were dancing. 'She frightens him, you know. She told him that

when she marries Jean-Marc, he'll have to go back to
Paris and live with his mother. I told him not to be such
a wet, but I think he's worried about Christmas. He
says his mother wouldn't let him come to England.'

Liz absorbed the information—another black mark
against Jean-Marc, although she was inclined to absolve
him. He probably didn't know anything about it. She
drank her Coke and joked with Ham, gradually
drawing Louis into the conversation until she saw, with
relief, the dead look leave his dark eyes. There were
several things about this set-up she couldn't understand.

When she had first discovered Louis' actual
relationship, that he had a mother living in Paris, she
had naturally assumed the boy was here on holiday and
that he would be returning when school restarted—she
was well aware that a great many Parisians made a
fetish of fresh air, leaving the city in droves at the
beginning of the annual holiday, and where it wasn't
possible for the parents to take the children, the kids
went to summer camps, so it was natural that Louis
should be here during August. A relative with a place in
the country was infinitely preferable to the regimentation of the average *colonie de vacances*. But Louis, from
what she could gather, was at Dieudonné on a
permanent basis, and this she couldn't understand,
not unless his mother was an invalid; she could think of
no other reason why he should have been brought to
live here where there was only an old housekeeper to
care for him.

'May I have this dance, Liz?' That was Jean-Marc
from behind her and for a moment, it didn't sink in, she
was too busy with her thoughts. She turned her head,
saw him, but it didn't register. 'This dance,' he insisted,
and slowly Liz came back to the present—the little gilt

chairs, the polished gleam of the floor and the four-piece band playing a waltz.

'Oh—er—yes.' She rose to her feet and surrendered to the inevitable. After all, it was what she was here for—a shield and buckler, she smiled wryly to herself as she saw Marie-France's glittering eyes following them round the floor. 'You're holding me too tightly again,' she hissed.

'Just giving the right impression,' Jean-Marc explained gravely.

'The wrong impression,' she contradicted, 'I've no intention of leaving here with my reputation in shreds, and that's what'll happen if you go on the way you're going. There are other women in the room, you know, so choose one of those next time—I'd rather stay with Ham and Louis, I don't think they're having much fun.' He paid no attention to her snappish tone, merely pulled her even closer so that she could have cried with vexation, and at the first break in the music, she pulled herself out of his arm.

'Find yourself another partner!' she stormed in a whisper while her face continued to smile. 'I'm going to the ladies' room,' and she threaded her way through couples with a red mist of anger floating before her eyes.

The ladies' room was a cool, quiet haven, and Liz turned on the cold tap over one of the handbasins to let the water trickle over her wrists. After a few seconds, she started to regain control over her temper and cool down. She was playing this all wrong. Hadn't she decided on a light, humorous approach, and what did it matter what anybody thought? She would soon be gone and never see this place or the people in it again, except for one very swift visit when she came to pick up Ham to take him back to England. She began to plan that visit, it would be of the lightning variety. She would drive up from Provence, stay at a hotel in Tours overnight, drive down here early in the morning and, with having to get to Le Havre the same day to catch the late ferry, she would have no time for anything more than 'Hello' and 'goodbye'. Having come to this decision, she felt calmer, and walked across to the vanity table where she seated herself on a stool and started to repair her make-up.

'So! You come to my party and make a spectacle of yourself!' Liz's hand jerked and sent the lipstick smearing across her cheek as she looked at Marie-France's reflection in the mirror. The girl was in a rage of disappointment, her eyes were glittering and her face was devoid of colour except for two spots of bright red high on her cheekbones. She was too angry even to speak English, and Liz found she didn't care if her French was a bit halting. The wench was a termagant, a spoiled little Madam. She deserved a set-down.

Carefully she pulled a tissue from her flat little bag and wiped the stain from her cheek. 'I beg your pardon, *mademoiselle*,' she said it icily, surprised to find the French tripping easily from her tongue; she had been so sure she would be stumbling, searching for words. 'You thought I was somebody else, perhaps?'

'There is no mistake,' the girl leaned closer so that her reflected face was just over Liz's shoulder. 'I speak to you, *madame*. You have ruined my party! I wish you to leave immediately.'

'Then you'll have to ask Monsieur St Clair to leave as well,' Liz said coolly, 'because I assure you, I have no intention of walking five kilometres back to Dieudonné, not in these,' and she waggled her foot to draw attention to her high-heeled sandals. She raised her eyes to the mirror and watched the girl's expression of dismay and chagrin. 'It's not so easy, is it?' she murmured in her best schoolteacher's manner, cool and indifferent, but she was neither cool nor indifferent. She didn't like hurting people, least of all this young girl— she didn't want to hurt her, but what else could she do? 'Monsieur St Clair brought me here this evening, so he'll have the good manners to take me back together with Louis and my nephew. If I did as you suggest and left, he would merely come after me.'

'Tonight,' Marie-France said it as though she was challenging fate to prove her wrong, 'tonight, Jean-Marc will ask me to marry him—it's all arranged.'

'Then I'll have to stay, won't I?' Liz looked coldly at the girl's mirrored reflection. 'He can hardly do that if he's driving me back to Dieudonné, and besides, I shall be the first to wish you both every happiness.' And she transfered her attention to repairing her lipstick, surprised to find her hand was quite steady.

'We shan't need your good wishes, *madame*!' Marie-France was shaking with temper. 'Not yours nor any of the other women of your kind. Jean-Marc has finished with those now, he will have me. Oh, I know what you are, but I won't let you spoil things for me. You'll leave Dieudonné, I promise you that. You should do as I say and go, but I can see you expect him to marry you, so I shall arrange things, and it will not be pleasant for you. You'll wish you had never come here!' and like a small, redheaded whirlwind, she dashed back to the ballroom.

Liz followed her, but more slowly. She was shaking with the effort she had made to control her temper, and somehow she put the unpleasant little scene down to Jean-Marc's account. How dared he leave her open to this kind of insulting behaviour! Of Marie-France's final threat, she thought no more, dismissing it as a young girl's hysterical outburst—all her venom was concentrated on Jean-Marc. She felt smirched and humiliated. 'Women of your kind' the girl had said, lumping her, Liz Fellowes, in with Jean-Marc's other female friends—and she didn't need it spelled out to tell her what sort of women they were.

She wished Bev was here, she desperately needed a shoulder to cry on, but she could hardly remember what he looked like; only that he was kind and considerate and that he had loved her. She felt tears starting in her eyes and pulled herself together. It was no good wishing for what she couldn't have, and if Bev had indeed been here, none of this would have happened. She wouldn't have been trying to reach Avignon, or if she had, Bev would have been driving and he wouldn't have run into that tree.

Liz came out of her dream to find Jean-Marc at her elbow. 'You won't mind, Liz, if we leave now,' his glance slid to the end of the room where Louis was dozing on a chair. 'I don't know whether it's tiredness or boredom, but Louis is asleep. We'd better take him home.'

'He's been sick,' Ham broke in, 'and we've been looking for you everywhere.'

'That's all I need!' she snapped. 'No,' she swung round on Jean-Marc, her eyes glowing with temper, 'I hear you have a commitment to make tonight, so if you wish to stay for it, I can manage to drive your car, I think, and as for myself, I can't get away from here quickly enough. I daresay you can hitch a lift with somebody, and if not, you're old enough and strong enough to damn well walk!'

'A commitment?' He raised his eyebrows and his lips quirked into a disillusioned smile. 'Marie-France has been talking, I see, but I told you, I've nothing like that in mind.'

'Then tell her!' Liz was at the end of her tether. 'She's the one with the wires crossed, not me.'

# CHAPTER FIVE

Liz spent an uncomfortable night wishing she'd never been born. The stark misery in Marie-France's eyes when they made their early farewells haunted her, but the malicious venom that replaced the misery was worse. The girl's eyes had promised an unpleasant triumph which had made Liz feel sick to her stomach with a sense of impending catastrophe and she couldn't think what it could be. She tried to dismiss it as imagination, but it coloured her dreams into fantastic nightmares where Ham was hurt, Louis had run away and trees, cars and a thousand other obstacles barred her road to Avignon while Jean-Marc sat laughing at her like the devil he really was.

She went down to the kitchen at breakfast time, but only to snatch a quick cup of coffee and retreated to the safety of her room at the first opportunity, although she had no fear of meeting Jean-Marc. It was Sunday morning, and she had learned that on Sundays he took over the milking to give the cowman the morning off. But she didn't feel like talking to anybody and flared with indignation when, later, Ham and Louis came bursting in. Louis was quite recovered from his bout of sickness which, the boys admitted, had been caused by a competition—who could drink the most cans of Coke in the shortest time.

'I'm having a quiet morning,' she growled at them, unable to work up a good snarl because of their evident excitement.

'That's all right,' Ham nodded, and behind him, Louis copied the gesture. 'We just came to tell you that we're having an early lunch and then we're all going to Chenonceau *and* Chaumont. That's two chateaux in one day, like the guide book says. It's got something to do with a lady called Diane de Poitiers, she lived in both of them, you see, so we mustn't be late starting off, otherwise we'll miss the the Son et Lumière performance.'

'Don't you think I've seen enough chateaux?' Liz demanded acidly.

'Enough?' Ham was outraged. 'Of course not! Today will only make five, and there are dozens, but Jean-Marc said Chenonceau was the most beautiful of them all, and I'm going to wear my kilt because I want you to take lots of snaps. I have to have something to show the kids in school, or they'll never believe me.'

'Then clear off while I find something to wear,' Liz ordered ungraciously. 'I suppose jeans and a tee-shirt won't do?'

' 'Course not!' Ham was shocked. 'It's Sunday!' And he and Louis went off about their private business while Liz inspected her sparse wardrobe. Ham was quite right about its being Sunday, which meant she'd been here a week, and already it felt as though she'd never known anywhere else. A faint dew of perspiration broke out on her forehead and upper lip as she contemplated the possibility that she might be stuck here for another week. It sent a shudder down her spine and she tried to block it off into an unused part of her mind while she flicked through the pitifully few hangers in the vast wardrobe.

She finally decided on a pink striped silk blouse and a white pleated skirt; it would be cooler than denim and the skirt was of a man-made fibre that washed, dripped dry and needed no pressing. She regretted sacrificing the silk shirt which she had brought along to eke out evening wear in hotels—it was bothersome, needing pressing, but perhaps Berthe would let her use an iron. . . . She took both garments and hung them in the bathroom while she had a quite unnecessary bath—and her white sandals would do. All that decided, she clambered out of the bath, rubbed herself dry and then, wrapped in a long bathrobe she'd found on a hook behind the door, sat herself down on the chair by the window and tried to work up a little enthusiasm for a paperback novel she had brought with her.

All in all it was an exhausting day—first Chenonceau which was beautiful, with the white arches of the river gallery reflected in the slow, sunlit waters of the river Cher, then on to Chaumont, grey and grim, where Diane de Poitiers, who was responsible for a lot of the beauty of Chenonceau, had been sent when her royal protector Henry II died, and then later at night, the stop at Azay le Rideau for the final Son et Lumière performance. Liz staggered up to bed that night and came down to breakfast the next morning with one resolution in her mind.

'No more chateaux!' She collared Ham's list of further ancient monuments and ripped it to pieces, sprinkling the bits in his empty cereal bowl, and when he opened his mouth to protest, 'Make yourself another list, I've had enough. Yes, I know there are lots more, but today I'm going no more than ten kilometres in any direction from this house. I'm tired!'

Louis, now much more forthcoming, solved the problem of how to keep his friend and his friend's aunt happy.

'We could go to the small vineyard after *déjeuner*,' he suggested. 'There's a chateau there and it's only a very little way from here. It's not a real chateau, only the ruins of an old castle, but it's a good place for a picnic and a good place to play. A long time ago I used to go there and pretend I was defending it from my enemies.'

'You're sure about that, Louis?' Liz looked and sounded relieved. 'There won't be miles of corridors that hurt my feet, rooms full of antique furniture or even painted ceilings that give me a stiff neck from looking up at them?'

'A few pieces of old wall only, Madame Liz,' Louis assured her. 'All covered now with grass on an open place on top of the hill. I think you will like it.'

'Then that's where we'll go,' she grinned at the two boys. 'Where's Jean-Marc, so we can tell him about the change of plan—that he won't have to drive us to Villandry?' And she glanced around as though she expected to find him hiding behind a kitchen chair.

'Down at the farm.' Both boys spoke simultaneously, one in French the other in English, and Ham went on, 'He's doing something with the plumber and the central heating radiators, but he said he wouldn't be long.'

Jean-Marc—she thought about him; she seemed to be doing quite a lot of that nowadays—being suspicious about exactly what he meant when he said something—searching for hidden meanings, but she had to admit that yesterday had been much better. He had treated her in a normal, friendly fashion and not made one pass at her as though he now thought the matter of Marie-France was settled and he no longer needed a shield. That was what it had all been about, Liz decided. He had tried to set up a little romance with her to put the girl off, and when Liz had refused to co-operate, he had appealed to her better nature. Liz remembered the hard green of the girl's eyes and wished him well. If he thought everything was settled, he couldn't be more mistaken—it would take more than a few dances to stop the doctor's young daughter. And there was the matter of the girl's threat, but he didn't know anything about that. She hoped she'd be well on the way to Avignon before Marie-France got her second breath!

Liz sent the boys out to play, with strict orders to change into picnic clothes before lunch, explained to Berthe that only a small quantity of food would be required for the afternoon, and then went to escape upstairs, but Jean-Marc was waiting for her before she had her foot on the first stair. 'Good morning, Liz. You slept well?'

'Yes, thank you,' she answered coolly—nobody was going to take any more liberties with her. 'We're going to an old ruin near your vine-yard after lunch. Louis says it's not far, so would there be enough bicycles to go round? I'm in need of some fresh air.'

'There are enough bicycles and I agree with you. It'll be a pleasant change; not so boring.'

'You've been listening at keyholes!' she accused.

'No,' he smiled down at her. 'Merely watching your face at that interminable Son et Lumière performance. You have a very expressive face when you don't realise you're being watched.'

'That's as maybe,' and at his slight frown of incomprehension, she smiled and sped up the stairs. His English was excellent, but she was glad she'd caught him out with one idiomatic phrase.

'What does that mean?' he called after her, and reaching the top, she looked down over the banisters and poked out her tongue. 'Work it out for yourself,' she called back. 'But I don't advise looking it up in a dictionary!'

Leaving the four bicycles propped against some small trees at the side of the narrow country road, Liz watched the two boys gallop ahead with the picnic basket and the cold box while she and Jean-Marc began a more leisurely climb up the narrow path which wound between the terraced ranks of vines. The grapes were already formed, hanging like bunches of hard green beads everywhere, defying the poor-looking soil which didn't seem capable of supporting life, never mind a crop of grapes. She said so, using the words as an excuse to stop halfway; the sun was hot, the path was steep and she was tired already. Jean-Marc swept an arm about her waist and started hauling her upwards while he explained.

'These grapes, these vines are the direct descendants of the original vines planted here in the fourteenth century. We've tried to grow them elsewhere, but they don't thrive. Here is where they belong, and they're quite different from the grapes we grow on ground we have a little further up the river. Those we send to the caves and bottling plant, which is a co-operative; all the must from this area goes there, but this hillside is on its own and we make our own special wine from them. We have here quality, but there will never be quantity, so we keep most if it for ourselves.'

Liz dropped on to the short turf which covered the top of the hill and reached into the cold box for a can of lemonade. 'Thirsty work,' she murmured. 'Was that a chateau at one time?' and she gestured to the tumbled mass of stone, now partly overgrown, where Ham and Louis were running mad and yelling like a couple of Red Indians.

'A fortified place,' he corrected, and dropped down beside her. 'And a very uncomfortable one, I should imagine—there's no trace of a well up here. Later on, when times became more settled, the de Villiers built themselves a more comfortable home—you've seen it in the little town. Now it's the Hotel de Ville in Villiers.'

'All candidates for the guillotine, I suppose?'

'Not at all,' Jean-Marc chuckled. 'The de Villiers had their ears to the ground and escaped into Italy before the Terror started claiming victims here, and they only came back when Napoleon offered an amnesty to anybody willing to serve in his armies. They couldn't have their chateau back, it had become the property of the State, but they were given some land and they built themselves a small one.'

'And lived happily ever after until the family died out, I suppose,' Liz finished the story for him.

'Uh-uh,' he shook his head. 'It wasn't any fairy story, Liz. The de Villiers were good soldiers but dreadful farmers, and when Napoleon fell, they lost nearly everything, but they did seem indestructible, in their way. When Napoleon the Third took over, back came the de Villiers as big men in the government, they sold their land and the house became a holiday home for them. But by the end of the first world war, there wasn't one of the family left and it was abandoned. When my father bought it, it was in a bad state of repair—nobody had lived in it for years, the roof leaked, plaster was falling off the walls, the windows were broken, the woodwork was rotting and the whole place was full of damp, mice and rats. It should have been pulled down.'

'A hard job getting it back into order again.' Liz gulped thirstily at her lemonade.

'And an expensive one,' he said grimly. 'It cost a fortune to repair and refurnish with the correct period pieces, although quite a lot are modern reproductions, and it costs another fortune to run. Just keeping it warm and dry in the winter takes over half the profits from the farm. That's why we're leaving it.' He reached out a lazy hand and tapped her wrist. 'That watch, Liz, it's too big for you. It makes your arm look like a stick and your hand like a bird's claw.'

Liz touched the big face with gentle fingers, 'It was Bev's, my husband's,' she muttered, wishing he'd go on talking about houses or anything that didn't hurt, and she rooted in her shoulder bag to find the sunglasses which would hide her face from him. 'Are the boys all right?'

'Perfectly, can't you hear them?' And listening, she could. There was Ham's noisy yell, Louis' gay laugh, the sound of a ball thudding—nothing to worry about there. Marcie always said that the time to be anxious was when Ham couldn't be heard. 'If he's silent, he's up to something,' that was her sister's standard, and she repeated it parrot fashion.

'My sister says that as long as they're making a noise that's intolerable, there's nothing wrong.'

Jean-Marc slid a glance at her. 'Until now, I've never heard Louis making a noise, he's generally very quiet.'

Liz took this as a slight on her nephew. 'You're suggesting that Ham's leading him into bad ways?' she demanded with the light of battle in her eyes. 'Let me tell you. . . .'

'No, don't,' he gave her a charming smile. 'I'm only saying that, until now. Louis has been like a mouse about the place, almost as though he didn't wish to be noticed.'

Liz shrugged. 'Probably something to do with moving about,' she suggested mildly. 'I mean, his mother takes him to live in Paris, then you bring him here—Oh, don't mind me. I've been a schoolteacher, remember, and there's not one of us who, after a year, doesn't think herself or himself an expert in child psychology—but honestly, children from unsettled homes are often quiet; that's an observation, not an opinion. But I don't think you need worry about Louis being too quiet, not any longer. After Ham goes home, you'll probably have to wear ear muffs to cut out the noise.'

'Then that's Louis settled, he's not a mass of inhibitions after all.' Jean-Marc relaxed and tried to light a cigarette while flat on his back; it was a little while before he succeeded. 'So the only other person we have to straighten out is you, Liz.'

'Me?' She pushed her sun-specs more firmly on to her nose and glared at him through the smoked lenses. 'Now you're being just as bad as my sister,' she snapped. 'She's always trying to interfere with my life, but I can excuse her, she's family. You, I can't excuse. My private life has nothing to do with you, and I'll thank you to remember that! I won't take interference from anybody.'

'Not even from a friend?'

'Ha!' she snorted. 'A fine friend you are—practically keeping me here against my will. . . .'

'Not against your will,' Jean-Marc said gently. 'If you'd been truly determined to go, you'd have gone and to hell with Ham, the car, anything.'

'How could I?' she flared. 'I've no transport and my face was a mess—besides, I didn't feel too well. The accident must have shaken me up more than I thought.'

'Excuses, excuses,' he baited her. 'You could have gone and you know it. In France, as in England, we have things that run on rails, you call them trains. You said you were desperate to get to Avignon, but you know there's nothing for you there, although you won't admit it.' He ground out the half-smoked cigarette on a flat stone and lay back, putting his hands behind his head and closing his eyes. 'Liz,' he spoke softly but every word was clear, 'why don't you try to forget, look to the future instead of living in the past?'

'Because I'm perfectly happy as I am,' she snapped. 'I like remembering and I don't think you've any business interfering with my private life; not you, not Marcie, not anybody, because none of you know. Bev and I,' her lips curved in a small reminiscent smile, 'we'd been together ever since we were small, we lived next to next in the same terrace. We played together, we did everything together. Maybe it wouldn't have been so bad if we'd met when we were grown up, only known each other a couple of years, but I remember the first time we decided to get married—I was eight and Bev was ten. I was in love with him then.'

'Nonsense!' Jean-Marc lit another cigarette. 'Remember what you told me about Marie-France, that she'd grow out of it? Me, I don't think this love you had was so wonderful.'

'It was!' Liz almost shouted it, the hurt of what he'd said went so deep that she turned towards him where he lay on the short turf, his eyes slitted against the bright sunlight. Her own eyes flashed with anger and her voice, when the words came at last, was a trifle shrill. 'You know nothing about it—and I *do* mean nothing! So you'll excuse me if I don't put any value on your opinion and tell you to mind your own business.

You've got plenty on your plate without bothering about mine!'

'Now why should my opinion be worthless?' He didn't turn his head, he simply kept staring up at the sky. 'I'm older than you, at least ten years, and there's little anybody can tell me about human nature—and I tell you, you can't live the rest of your life on a memory. Life's ahead of you, it's for living, not for burying yourself in somebody else's grave. You've lost your man, so—there are other men.'

Liz went cold with anger and the words dripped from her tongue, corrosive as acid, saying things she had never said to anybody before—it was as though a dam had burst and she could no longer control the flow.

'Men!' She spat the word. 'Oh yes, there are thousands of men! But you don't know the half of it. I'm a widow, remember,' her lips stretched in a wide, bitter smile. 'Widows are a race apart—we aren't treated as ordinary women. We don't need to be courted, we have no maidenly hesitation because we've been there before. All I've had from those men are insults—and that includes yours! And I'd only been here a couple of days at that, you hardly knew me.'

'I wasn't insulting you,' he replied imperturbably. 'I was attracted to you and, to be blunt, I thought it was a mutual thing—besides,' his cheeks creased in a smile of reminiscence, 'you were very upset about your car, I thought you should have something else to think about. . . .'

'. . . Oh, how noble and self-sacrificing you are!' she broke in on him fiercely. 'Putting yourself out like that just to distract my mind!' The words rolled off her tongue, larded with sarcasm, and she pushed her sunglasses more firmly on to her nose and looked sightlessly to where Ham and Louis were chasing each other around the remnants of the old walls, well out of hearing range.

'That's right.' For the first time since she had met him, Jean-Marc sounded angry and she took a swift glance at his face, but it was set in its usual lines of sardonic disillusion. A mask, she thought, and who was to tell what went on behind it, but he was angry, it was there in the harsh abrasiveness of his voice. 'Hide behind those glasses, Liz,' he continued. 'I think that's a sign you're not as sure of yourself and your emotions as you'd like me to think—but harking back to that episode where you say I insulted you; that's not quite true, is it? You knew it was going to happen, you had the signs well in advance. You could have stopped me— or do you think I'm the cave man type? I assure you I'm not; neither am I a young boy to tumble a girl behind a hedge and not mind the discomfort. *Mon dieu*,' he lapsed into swift French, 'the bed hadn't been properly aired!'

It was such an anticlimax that Liz found herself hooting with laughter, and he raised an eyebrow. 'I've said something amusing?'

'N-no,' she gulped, all her nastiness forgotten. 'I'd forgotten how practical the French are, that's all. No lovemaking unless the scene is complete in every detail, even to having the bed aired!'

'And,' he began to sound virtuous, 'I stopped as soon as you wished me to. I thought it a very pleasant first encounter. . . .'

The nastiness returned in full force and Liz writhed with indignation. 'First encounter? My God, you've got a nerve! Is that why you think I've been staying on here, for a repeat performance? The next thing you'll be telling me is that we're soulmates or some other trivial nonsense. That might go down very well with your other lady friends—and I bet you've had plenty—but it cuts no ice with me. I've heard that sort of thing too many times before and I know exactly what it's worth!'

'There have been some,' he admitted gravely. 'I'm thirty-six and I'm not a monk; besides, every man has to learn, otherwise there'd be a lot of unhappy and unsatisfied wives. I don't suppose your own husband came to you a virgin.'

'That's enough!' Liz struggled to her knees. 'I won't sit here and listen to another word. You've no right—I think this conversation's been disgusting—I won't have my private affairs pried into! Speaking to me like that—saying those things. . . .'

Jean-Marc rolled over on to his side, putting out a lazy arm to catch her about the hips and pull her off balance so that she tumbled beside him. As though she'd been hypnotised into immobility, she did nothing while he pulled off her sunglasses, dropping them on the turf, and she watched unmoving as he rolled over completely, pulling her half way beneath him.

'Was this what it was like, Liz?' It was only a murmur and she felt the warm breath of the words against her lips before his mouth was on hers. It wasn't a clumsy, hurried kiss and there was nothing greedy about it; heaven knew she'd had enough of those in the last two years—fighting them off in taxis and struggling away from them at the door of her flat.

Her dazed mind could recognise a tender giving from his mouth to hers, a giving that sought but didn't demand a response. She whimpered deep in her throat as she tried to control an almost involuntary response, while something hot and sweet burst into life inside her, flooding her with a warmth that made all her bones turn to water—and then it was easy. Her arms slid about his shoulders, her mouth parted beneath his and when she felt his hand at her breast, the fingers caressing, she moaned softly and felt her body arch to meet his.

She was drowning in an age of sweetness and delight, an immeasurable time when everything about her was a golden haze and hunger clawed at her stomach, driving her on. The black curls were crisp against her fingers, the smell of him was in her nostrils, and when she slid her hand into the open neck of his shirt, his skin was like satin under her fingers, and it only stopped when he raised his head. Even then, she could sense his reluctance to break the contact.

'Was it like that?' he asked, and she looked at him, able to see him clearly for the first time. She saw his eyes beneath the heavy lids and the long, curling lashes—the pupils distended until the grey irises were only a narrow ring of light around enormous black depths; depths which were drawing her in to drown, to be a mindless body, willing, wanton. She reacted violently, pushing him away from her with frantic hands, grabbing at her glasses and scrambling to her feet. Jean-Marc rose as well, straightening his tumbled hair and breathing rather quickly.

'It's all right, Liz. The boys are too far away to have seen, they're well over on the other side, out of sight.'

Her humiliation was complete; she hadn't even given a thought to Ham and Louis but he had. Oh, *he* had! He'd been able to think about reasonable things, he hadn't been a mindless puppet—and she beat away his hands furiously before she raced away across the flat ground and down the winding path between the serried rows of vines.

She was sobbing as she fled, doing up the buttons of her shirt with shaking fingers. *No!* It hadn't been anything like that! She swiftly shut out memories. It had been better, better, *better*! There hadn't been anything so arrogantly sexual, she hadn't felt as though she was lost. With Bev, she had always been in control of herself, she had been safe! That was how it had been, how it should be—she hadn't drowned in a sea of feverish delight, wanting more and more until she was no longer an individual, only part of something bigger which scared her stiff while it beckoned enticingly.

At the bottom of the hill, she halted a moment to find her bearings and to tie a scarf about her head, binding back the sweep of hair which somehow had escaped the neat ponytail and was flying about her shoulders. The sobs were hard and dry in her throat, hurting her and making her gasp for breath as she ran to the small clump of trees where they had left the bicycles. She pushed the boys' aside and pulled her own from the pile to wheel it out on to the road and mount it, then, head down, she pedalled furiously along the road back to Dieudonné.

Shame rode with her, shame that she could have forgotten every bit of the self-respect she held so dear, and she castigated herself with every turn of the pedals. She had heard men talking before, Bev had been a member of a Rugby club, and among those extroverts remarks flew freely, especially after a good game and a lot of beer removed their inhibitions. 'A good lay' and 'An easy lay', those were the sort of expressions used, and that was what she would have been called—what she would have been if she'd lost control completely. She couldn't even think in a straight line any more, and the road blurred before her eyes as she raised a hand to dash the tears from them.

By the time she reached Dieudonné, her mind was made up—she knew what she had to do. Now that she was a bit calmer, she could get things into a more sane perspective. Nothing would have happened this afternoon up on the hill, Jean-Marc wouldn't have let it—after all, a man who objected to an unaired bed wouldn't even consider a sunlit hillside with two young boys within call, but she would have to go, and at once. A time might come when Jean-Marc would decide the conditions were favourable, and she knew now that the attraction between them was too strong for her to risk being subjected to it again.

She would go straight upstairs and pack her case: by that time, the boys should be back and she could say goodbye to them before she phoned for a taxi to take her into Angers. From there, she would catch the first train into Tours, and it didn't matter if she could get no further today. Tours would be far enough. Then after a night's sleep in a hotel, she would find the best, the quickest way to Avignon. There, surrounded by memories of Bev, she would be safe. This was what she should have done right at the beginning, or as soon as Jean-Marc had made his first pass at her.

But he hadn't followed that pass up and Liz had relaxed her guard, vaguely hoping he was different. Different! She snorted at her own stupidity. There were no different men, they were all the same, except Bev, and she would never find his like again. Dear Bev—a bit tonguetied and loath to talk about intimate things even after they were married. He would never have said the things Jean-Marc had said; he not only loved her, he respected her!

Planning like this was good for her, it steadied her nerves and she could give the appearance of calm composure. She dropped the bike on its side on the grass verge and set about going into the house. She had to be cool, and she was so intent on that, that she walked straight past a red Porsche without even noticing it. The ice was back around her in a layer about a foot thick, and she hoped its chill would eventually permeate into the little hot core in her stomach; the only place where the fire Jean-Marc had lit still remained alive. She went in through the big doors which, as usual, were standing ajar and hurried to the staircase, wondering wryly how he was coping with the boys. Viciously, she hoped they were giving him a lot of trouble!

'B'jour, madame,' came a soft, sweet voice from above her, and Liz paused with one foot on the bottom step as she looked up the staircase. The sweet voice continued, 'I think you are very wise to have come back early, there is a storm coming. I hope Jean-Marc won't let my little Louis get wet.'

The woman coming down the stairs was perfection. Liz had always considered herself a bit more than reasonably good-looking, but here was beauty, and she became aware of untidy hair where she had snatched off her scarf, smears of dust and a grass stain or two on her skirt and sandals; she was also hot. As a cloud of perfume enveloped her, she found herself praying that her deodorant was working as well as the blurb on the bottle said it would.

'Madame St Clair?' Liz took in everything in one swift, comprehensive glance. The lady was as small and dainty as a Dresden shepherdess. The cloud of dark hair drawn back softly from a small, heartshaped face spoke of superb cutting and the chignon effect was just what she had always wanted for herself and never been able to achieve. The large, velvety soft eyes, fringed with long black lashes, looked down at her and there was a sad, almost regretful expression in them.

'Call me Vivienne, please,' a small, very white hand gestured to the impeccably cut two-piece in thin black silk. 'Berthe has been telling me about you and I feel a bond between us.' The English was good, although nowhere near as good as Jean-Marc's. The accent was more pronounced and there was more hesitation in the choice of words, but the soft, husky voice excused it all, and Liz felt herself going under a spell of mild hypnosis. Vivienne St Clair gestured at her own wedding-ring and then looked at Liz's. 'We've both suffered, no? Suffering always creates a bond.' She came down the remaining stairs to halt on the step above Liz's, which brought their eyes nearly on the same level but not quite; Madame St Clair evidently preferred to look down on people.

'Berthe is now making me tea,' she continued smoothly. 'I so like your English tea, more refreshing than coffee. When you have tidied yourself, it will be waiting in the *salon*—please join me there.'

'And that's telling you you're a disgusting object to look at,' Liz muttered to herself as she went on up the stairs. In the bedroom, she speculated on the advisability of carrying on with her new-made plans, but she came to the conclusion that so much haste was no longer necessary. Tomorrow would do just as well, and in any case, she could run down to the farm early and see if her car was ready. It didn't matter to her what colour it was as long as it was roadworthy, she would cheerfully drive round France with only grey undercoat on the wings and bonnet as long as she could go!

Meanwhile, she had better make herself presentable and join her hostess for tea. Louis' mother had come as a bit of a shock to her, she wasn't what Liz had expected. She had been expecting a much older woman or, at least, a woman who looked much older. Vivienne St Clair didn't look a day over twenty-five or six, while common sense told Liz she must be at least thirty-two, if not older, and at first glance, which was all she had had so far, Liz didn't think Madame St Clair looked the sort of woman who would abandon her son or even let somebody else bring him up. She dismissed the air of fragility with a sniff, together with the gentleness. In her opinion—she knew it wasn't worth much, being based on only a few seconds' acquaintance and a couple of sentences—but her immediate impression had been of a very determined lady.

On the other hand, it wasn't right to be swayed by snap judgments, not when she might have been influenced by anything Jean-Marc had said. She cast her mind back, trying to remember what he *had* said about his stepmother, but apart from the fact that she was beautiful and had been an *assistante* at the infants' school, he had said nothing else. He hadn't even implied that Vivienne had married his father for money.

Liz struggled her showered body into a two-year-old cotton dress and bent to the mirror to pin back her hair—all the same, whether Jean-Marc had said anything or nothing, she decided to rely on her own first impressions, which weren't favourable. 'And,' she addressed her reflection as she swept a powder puff over her face and settled the sunglasses firmly on her nose, 'it's probably sheer jealousy on your part, my girl. You just can't stand the slender, young Elizabeth Taylor type. They make you look like a starved carthorse!'

'You intend to stay here for the entire month?' Vivienne raised the heavy silver teapot and poured a pale stream into each of the fragile cups. Liz caught sight of the teabag tags dangling from the lid and sighed with regret. Her first cup of tea in France, excluding the one she'd had on the night of the accident—that one didn't count—and it wasn't going to be English tea. From the look of it, it was going to taste like hot water flavoured with sugar and milk.

'No.' She accepted the cup quietly and added a little sugar; she didn't think it would stand milk. 'I'm going on to Avignon. I would have been there already but for an unfortunate accident with the car.'

Vivienne nodded understandingly and sipped delicately like a cat at a saucer of cream. 'The traffic nowadays—one has only to lose one's concentration for a second. . . . You were not too badly hurt, I hope?'

Liz had been going to say the culprit wasn't another car but one of Jean-Marc's trees, but she decided against it. 'Nothing serious,' she waved aside her bumps and bruises as though they were of no importance. 'The car was the only casualty, I'm afraid it suffered badly, but it should be ready for the road any day now.'

'And Jean-Marc, he has been a good host? He's made you feel comfortable during your stay?'

At ths point, Liz decided she didn't care for Vivienne St Clair, in fact, she didn't like her. The woman made the hairs on the back of her neck bristle. She had always deplored people who took unreasonable dislikes to others on sight, but now it seemed she was one of them and she could not understand it, because it had never happened to her before. She usually got on very well with other women. Perhaps it was the gentle inquisition, the questions which weren't personal. She tried to imagine the reply if she had told any one of her acquaintances that she had had an accident in the car, and came up with the answer. They'd all say, 'Were you hurt, and how did it happen?' But not this woman. Liz smiled gently while she tried for a more charitable approach.

'Most comfortable,' she answered. 'I've really enjoyed my stay.'

# CHAPTER SIX

Liz examined her one decent dress, bemoaning fate and angry with herself for not carrying out her plan to pack and go. She had been in two minds after drinking tea with Louis' mother, but she had allowed the car to influence her more than she should have done. Bev had loved that car, so, if she could go to Avignon in it, she would be that much closer to him. And then, afterwards, she shouldn't have given way to the boys— but that was fate for you; one made plans, one should stick to them, be strong-minded, but she was a sucker for Ham's woebegone look and Louis' dark, worried eyes.

Ham had tapped on her door and came in, closely followed by Louis just as she had seated herself—in her underwear, covered decently by the cotton kimono and wondering if it was worth while doing anything special to her face.

'St Nazaire tomorrow,' Ham smiled widely at her. 'Jean-Marc says the boat'll be ready at nine,' and then he caught sight of her case, the lid open to disclose the neatly packed contents. 'You're not going, Liz? You can't, not now! You *have* to stay, otherwise it's going to be awful!'

'This has happened before!' Liz groaned. 'Every time I get ready to go, you and Louis charge in and tell me I can't. What's the matter now, for pity's sake? You know I can't stay here indefinitely, and now Louis' mother's arrived, you can list me as "not wanted on voyage".'

'Your car's not ready.' Ham's face was scarlet with embarrassment, which Liz took to mean that the readiness of the car wasn't of great importance to him. He had some other reason for wanting her here.

She swung herself round on the stool to face him. 'Come clean, my wee laddie—has your mum been laying down the law again, fusing the telephone wires between here and Richmond? What's the real reason? I promise you, if it's good, I'll have a rethink until my car's ready, but if it's your usual load of nonsense, I shall be on the first train out of Angers tomorrow morning.'

'If you go, Louis says we'll never be able to go anywhere!' Ham's scarlet face deepened to carmine, right the way down to the third button of his play-shirt. He looked at Louis and at the French boy's despairing grimace, his red face set in an expression of grim determination. 'You don't understand,' he muttered. 'It's Louis' mum!'

'Doesn't she want to go to St Nazaire tomorrow?' Liz raised an eyebrow.

'Oh, Louis says she'll go as long as it's only a little trip, because she always stays in her room until lunchtime and we'd hardly be able to go any distance at all because she'll want to come back early so's she can dress for dinner. That won't be the same either, because she'll have people coming or else she'll go out. Louis says it always hapens when she comes, he never goes anywhere, and we'll have to wear our best clothes all the time and read books—not comics—*Books!*'

'Good for you.' Liz was without pity.

'*Mais c'est vrai*, Madame Liz,' Louis piped up from behind her nephew. 'And poor Jean-Marc, he has worked so hard, but now he won't take the holiday. He will work at the farm all the time and my mother will say we must be quiet.'

'It'll spoil everything!' Ham was becoming strident and Liz shushed him. 'We had it all worked out,' he continued in a quieter voice. 'Didn't we, Louis? So you *must* stay, Liz, and it won't be for long, because Louis says his mum never stays for more than three or four days. That way, we'll be all right even if Jean-Marc does go off to the farm every day. We could go with you instead—and you remember, we had lots of fun on the buses.'

Liz looked at the two beseeching faces and her resolution crumbled. 'Very well, you've talked me into it—but no longer than Friday, I want to get away before the weekend and,' she became serious. 'I'll only take you if Louis' mother gives her permission—*and* you'll have to be good!'

'We will.' Ham breathed a sigh of relief and put a protecting arm about his friend's small shoulders while he murdered the French language.

'Say bong, Lewey—I told you, Liz isn't scared of anything or anybody, so come on and let's get this washing thing over. *Tu* can have *le bain avant* me.' By which Liz gathered that Ham was comforting his friend and giving him first turn in the bath as a consolation prize. She stifled hysterical laughter until they'd gone and then allowed her face to break into a broad smile while she concentrated on her make-up, giving herself a doe-eyed look which made her appear surprisingly demure, a morale booster and one she would need, having seen Vivienne's black silk travel wear.

Louis' mother would probably sweep in to dinner in black silk chiffon by Yves St Laurent, so Liz used a blusher sparingly and a slightly darker lipstick and gloss to compensate for the tricel knit, and was quite pleased with the result; even the chignon she had achieved with some difficulty and a lot of pins looked quite good. 'Cheer up, girl,' she comforted herself as she examined the seams of her stockings in the full-length mirror. 'Your legs are better, if only because they're longer.' Halfway down the stairs, she stopped while she wondered why she'd gone to all this trouble; it wasn't as though she was even faintly interested in what people thought. A matter of personal pride, she decided, which was a very stupid thing and she continued on with a faintly self-mocking smile on her face.

Vivienne's black silk chiffon wasn't by St Laurent, it was by Pierre Cardin, and it drifted about her small person like a cloud of darkness, relieved only by a triple string of pearls and some very hefty pearl and diamond rings; all obviously genuine. All this plus exquisite, hardly noticeable make-up and a perfume which was insidious rather than noticeable made Liz feel like something out of the bargain basement, but she conquered her reluctance and walked steadily down the length of the room to a small sideboard where Jean-Marc was dispensing drinks.

'Perrier menthe, Liz?' He turned to her with a lopsided smile and nodded her to a seat by the fire. 'It's non-alcoholic and you can always think of it as medicine.'

'Lovely!' Liz had thought she would be embarrassed at the sight of him, but the smile restored her self-confidence. He was making nothing of that frantic embrace up on the hill, so she would forget it too. Love, she knew; she had had the calm, gentle certainty of that with Bev, so what she had felt in Jean-Marc's arms wasn't love, only some sort of sexual drive with nothing of calm, gentleness or certainty about it. It was powerful, she admitted, like a river in full flood—but after the flood there was always a lot of broken stuff left stranded on the banks, not a fate she would appreciate. She pushed it to the back of her mind and after a nice smile at Vivienne, covered her thoughts with a layer of small talk.

'Ham and Louis said something about St Nazaire tomorrow, by boat. I think I'd like that, it's as well to see as much as possible before I have to leave.'

'But don't you think that's too far, Jean-Marc?' Vivienne made a little moue of distress. 'Much too far for my little Louis. It would take so long to get there and even longer to return; he'd be tired by afternoon and completely exhausted by dinnertime. He wouldn't be able to eat properly, and then the nightmares would start again.' She appealed to Liz, 'Don't you agree with me? My Louis isn't strong, he becomes tired very easily. You must have noticed this.'

Liz kept her expression noncommittal while she thought of the boundless energy which both Louis and Ham possessed. How they pedalled furiously down to Villiers each morning, swam all morning, pedalled back, ate everything in sight and then stood panting with anticipation for the next outing. Neither of the boys had shown the slightest sign of flagging so far as she could see—and this posed a problem. How could she say that Louis seemed to have the constitution of a horse? While she was making up her mind to murmur politely without saying anything, either one way or the other, Vivienne continued—apparently Liz's reply wasn't necessary.

'If he wants to go to St Nazaire, then we can go by car, so much less tiring and it will be quicker. We'll leave after lunch and we can be there in an hour and a half. That will give us an hour or so to show the English boy round the town, and we can be back here by six in the evening. . . .'

The soft, sweet voice went on and on. . . . Liz thought longingly of ear-plugs while she sipped at her drink and, out of the corner of her eye, watched Jean-Marc. He stood listening attentively, a faint, sardonic smile on his face, a smile that didn't reach his eyes, then Ham put his head around the *salon* door.

'Liz!' he yelled in a foghorn voice. 'Mum's on the phone, she wants to speak to you.'

It couldn't have been better timed, and Liz hurried off, feeling like a modern Joan of Arc who had been released from the stake just as the flames were licking round her ankles.

'Is that you, Liz?' Marcie sounded grumpy. 'You're still there, then?'

'What did you expect?' Liz glared at the telephone. 'I told you, the car's bust. I'm waiting here for it to be repaired.'

'Then you won't be going to Avignon?' Marcie's grumpiness vanished instantly. 'I mean, there won't be time, will there? How are you getting on with tall, dark and handsome?'

Liz evaded the question. 'More to the point, how are you? Did your op go off successfully?'

'Oh, that,' Marcie dismissed it airily. 'Never felt better, it's really you I was worried about. You haven't written and Ham's postcards never mentioned you, so I thought you must have gone on. Tell me, what's this Jean-Marc like?'

'Everything I ever dreamed of,' Liz said sarcastically. 'Be sensible, Marcie. He's only a chance acquaintance, there's no need for you to go into your moon, spoon and June thing. In any case, we didn't meet in very auspicious circumstances. It was his tree I bashed into. I *love* him for that, of course!'

'It's certainly a novel approach. Do you fancy him?'

'No,' Liz scowled at the phone. 'I'm hanging up now. . . .'

'No, don't do that,' her sister interrupted. 'Ham says that Louis' mother has just arrived. Doesn't she live there all the time?'

'No,' Liz said wearily. 'She lives in Paris—this is one of her flying visits.'

'Better and better. He's not married, his stepmother doesn't live with him. . . .'

Liz gritted her teeth. 'Shut up!' she said forcefully. 'I've told you time and time again, I'm not in the market, so go and start up your Romance Bureau with another client. If I *was* interested—which I'm not— listening to you would put me right off!' and she slammed down the phone with a clatter.

Back in the *salon*, Vivienne was no longer worrying herself and anybody who would listen about Louis' frailty, his fragility and ability to catch any disease going—she was now, with the aid of a small notebook and a tiny gold propelling pencil, trying to make out a few 'guests for dinner' lists. Unfortunately she was forced to reject every one of her selections, ending up with a blank page, and she smiled sadly at her stepson.

'Nearly everybody's on holiday,' she mourned, 'and I'm not used to dining en famille, it doesn't make for brilliant conversation—one is so restricted.'

'You'll bear with us for a couple of days, no doubt.' Jean-Marc was not forthcoming with an alternative to the en famille dinners, 'and in any case, Berthe is a good but plain cook, we couldn't ask her to do anything special for you.'

'And she's old!' Vivienne smiled ruefully. 'Truly, Jean-Marc, you're too kind to her. She should be retired—a small cottage, a little pension, it wouldn't cost you much.' They had been speaking in French and Liz missed his reply, as she missed most of the unstimulating conversation during dinner. She paid little attention to what she ate or drank, concentrating on Ham and Louis, both of whom seemed unnaturally subdued. Ham she could understand, he was wearing his party manners—'speak when you're spoken to and don't wolf everything in sight'—but Louis, she darted a swift glance at the boy—Louis, she couldn't understand.

Anyway, she comforted herself, none of what was going on was her business, so there was no need to interest herself in it, but her mouth curved into a tiny smile when, just as the meal was ending and the boys were starting to load their trolley, Jean-Marc instructed them to go straight to bed when they had finished their chores.

'We want an early start in the morning,' he told them seriously. 'Anybody who oversleeps will be left behind.'

So he wasn't paying any attention to Vivienne's objections! Liz mentally raised an eyebrow and almost missed the words he addressed to herself.

'You too, Liz, although I hope you won't be expecting anything superb in the way of water transport. We've put a new engine in the old tub so that it goes a little faster than it used to do, but there's not much comfort. It's the boat we use for fishing in the early spring when the shad come up the river, so it always smells of fish. It'll be a slow trip down to the coast and an even slower one back, but we should have an hour or so for you to investigate the old town. Berthe is packing food for us and there's a small galley aboard where we can make coffee or, if you prefer, tea.'

'It sounds delightful, and a most welcome change,' Liz heard herself manufacturing enthusiasm. 'I've always liked rivers and boats. It sounds as though it's going to be a lovely, lazy day and I shan't have to admire any antiquities.'

'You don't care for antiquities?' That was Vivienne's soft question as they left the dining-room and went back to the *salon*. 'You are the modern type, then, you prefer things plain and functional?'

'Not at all.' Liz shook her head as she made for a seat by the fire, holding out a slender foot to the blazing logs. She was grateful for the warmth of it and was regretting her cardigan which was doing nothing but lying on the end of the bed. She had thought she wouldn't need it, the day had been so sunny and hot. She kept her eyes on the fire and her face averted while her head spun in a crazy cartwheel. Was it only this afternoon she had been up on that hilltop with Jean-Marc and come running from there filled with shame at her uninhibited response? It seemed an age ago! And here she was now, behaving as though her world hadn't been turned upside down—looking at him, talking to him as though they were merely chance acquaintances.

This afternoon she had wanted to scratch his eyes out for what he had done to her, and now she was accepting a cup of coffee from him and thanking him as though she hadn't a care in the world. She shook her head at her own stupidity and went on with what she had been saying.

'There are a lot of drawbacks to the modern stuff,' —

Jean-Marc was quite right about this house being the devil to keep warm. The night mist from the river was creeping up, putting chill, clammy fingers on her—she shivered and went back to the drawbacks of modern furniture. 'I always find the drawers aren't big enough or deep enough. I suppose I'd like antiques better if I could see them being used as they were intended to be—not railed off for tourists to look at.'

She went on chatting madly, trying to overcome the feeling of depression which was stealing over her. There were undertones here she didn't understand—undertones which had been here when she arrived, but it was as if Vivienne was a catalyst for them. Now, they were so much deeper and more meaningful, but the meaning escaped her.

Vivienne carefully arranged her floating draperies as she sat in the chair opposite, looking like a little marquise out of her time, and a little smile played about her mouth.

'But you like this house, don't you?'

Liz smiled back and murmured without saying much. How could she say that, as a house, a showpiece, it was superb, but as a home, it rated zero for her? That she infinitely preferred the old farmhouse which felt warm and welcoming—still felt lived in though it had been empty for so long. She remembered her own home, when her parents had been alive and before Marcie had brought it up to date, large and shabby but friendly and full of laughter. She couldn't imagine this place ever being like that.

Fortunately, Jean-Marc started collecting coffee cups for refills, and Vivienne turned her attention to her stepson.

'You insist on this boat trip, *mon cher*?'

'I promised the boys, and you should know by now that I keep my promises.' He raised an eyebrow. 'Are we to have the pleasure of your company?'

Vivienne shrugged gracefully. 'So early in the morning,' she sighed, 'but what choice do I have? And it will be a long day. . . .' Her voice trailed away into incoherency.

'I'm sure you'll be able to force yourself,' he said gently.

Liz went upstairs to bed that night puzzling over what was, to her, very peculiar behaviour between members of a family. Coming as she did from a home where everybody had been very close, she failed to understand the lack of rapport between Vivienne and her son. Louis' mother gave the impression of being a careful parent, yet she hardly ever spoke to the boy and Louis kept as far away from his mother as possible. She recalled as much as she could of the relationship between Marcie and Ham, the only mother-and-son duo she knew about—really knew. Marcie made no pretence about being the perfect parent, she cuffed Ham when he was naughty, shouted when he made a mess, but Ham wasn't afraid of her.

The thought made Liz jerk upright in bed. That was it! Louis seemed to be afraid of his mother. As for Jean-Marc—well, it was difficult to tell what he was thinking; he didn't let anything show on the surface except a weary kind of cynicism and she, Liz, couldn't believe she had imagined the faint, sardonic note which had underlaid his every remark to his stepmother.

An hour later Liz was still thinking about it. Perhaps Jean-Marc hadn't approved of his father marrying a girl so young, maybe there was a little jealousy involved—he sounded as though he had loved his own mother dearly. And here she was, Liz Fellowes, doing the very thing she had decided not to do—interesting herself in other people's affairs. She turned on her side, hitched the pillow under her cheek and closed her eyes firmly, but her thoughts went on and on. It could be more than a little jealousy on the part of Jean-Marc and maybe she'd got it the wrong way round.

Hadn't he said all the young men were after the beautiful *'assistante'*, himself included? Maybe he had wanted her for himself and was chagrined that she had married his father instead of waiting for him. With a sigh of disgust at her growing involvement and her inability to clear her mind, Liz switched on the bedside light and scrambled out of bed to paw through the contents of her suitcase in search of her paperback, then scurried back to bed, to become immersed in the life of the young Merlin in Mary Stewart's, *the Crystal Cave*.

Vivienne appeared at the breakfast table on time and dressed for a day's sailing. She didn't have a nautical cap, but it was the only item missing from an otherwise complete seafaring ensemble. White matelot trousers, a cotton knit top in broad, horizontal stripes of navy and white; tiny rope-soled sandals and a navy blue reefer jacket over her arm.

Liz, in much washed and faded jeans topped with a candy pink tee-shirt, felt like something the cat had brought in and she was mortified to discover that, although when she stood next to Marcie, she made her sister look small—standing beside the small Frenchwoman had a quite different effect. Vivienne was so perfectly proportioned, she didn't give the appearance of being small; it was Liz herself who seemed to have grown to the dimensions of a rugby full-back; big and brawny with over-large hands and feet!

They all piled into a bigger car than Jean-Marc had driven before, a Matra which looked as though it was used to go to markets and for carrying things, and Liz, walking round it to get into the back seat with the boys, wrinkled her nose at a crumpled back bumper. Jean-Marc picked up her expression.

'Your car has priority,' he told her. 'This can wait. But I've noticed you haven't been to see it for a few days, you aren't marking its progress. Is your desire to get to Avignon waning?'

'Not in the least,' she answered cheerfully, although she avoided his eyes. 'Avignon's still my goal, and if the car's not roadworthy by Friday, I shall do as you suggested and take a train.'

'So much effort!' Without thinking, she raised her eyes to his and found them glinting at her wickedly. 'What's in Avignon, Liz, beside memories?'

'Armour,' she retorted promptly, a sparkle in her own blue eyes. 'And I need it, at least an inch thick and made of well tempered steel, if I'm dealing with you or any other flirt!'

'I never flirt!' He sounded indignant and she sniffed in a disbelieving fashion as he opened the door for her.

'You could have fooled me!' And then to the two boys who had spread themselves out over the width of the seat, 'Move over, lads, I'm too big to squeeze into that little space.'

'Not big,' came the murmur behind her, and then the door was closed on her and he finished it off through the open window. 'I'd prefer to say seductive, but you shouldn't fish for compliments.'

Liz flushed and gave all her attention to winding up the window while the two boys squeezed up, which wasn't an easy operation. They both had fishing rods which they refused to part with, not even into the empty space behind the seat where they could easily have kept their eyes on them, and then they all turned to watch Vivienne's approach, which rather resembled that of a model on a catwalk.

The Frenchwoman's face expressed reproach. 'Jean-Marc,' she semi scolded, 'you should have put our guest in front with you, she would have seen so much more.' She turned her head to Liz, smiling sweetly. 'I've seen it all before,' she remarked in a world-weary tone.

'I'm told it's only ten minutes' drive to the boat,' Liz said sturdily, 'so I shan't miss much, shall I?'

The boat proved to be an old yawl-rigged craft but fitted with an engine—the kind of boat which could be used for inshore fishing, and when she was aboard, Jean-Marc waved his hands to demonstrate.

'I told you it wasn't superb, but we do have the romance of sail on the journey down the river. Coming back, we'll reef the sail and rely on the engine to take us against the current.'

Liz, who was making an inspection of the tiny cabin and galley, poked her head out and chuckled. 'No, as you said, not superb. Sedate would be a better word, sedate and a bit broad in the beam—and it *does* smell of fish!' She watched as Ham and Louis scurried about on the old wooden landing stage, letting go the mooring lines before they skipped lightly aboard, and she watched as Jean-Marc hoisted the rust-red sail before she went to search for the Coke and Fanta which the boys were demanding.

It was a good day, and although they had little time to see much of St Nazaire, Liz enjoyed herself once she had decided to ignore Vivienne's air of acute boredom. The Frenchwoman disposed herself on a seat in front of the wheel-house, utilising every rug and cushion available to make herself comfortable, and she spoke only three times during the entire journey down river. The first was when Louis stumbled against her and put a distinctly grubby little hand on her white trousers— for which she scolded him, calling him a little peasant— the second time was when Liz offered a cup of coffee, which she declined, and on the third occasion, she yawned aloud and begged pardon for it.

Ham and Louis trailed fishing lines overboard without very much hope of catching anything but enthusiastically discussing what they would do with a fish if they had the good fortune to catch one, and Liz sat in the stern, watching the river banks slide past and listening to the soft slap of the water against the boat's stout wooden sides while she tried to get closer to Bev. But Bev seemed to be very far away, a whole lifetime away, and even though she touched the face of his watch, she couldn't bring him any nearer.

Jean-Marc saw her slightly distressed expression and turned his head to look at her fully. 'Sad thoughts, Liz?'

'No.' Her armour of composed coolness was back with her and her face was noncommittal. She manufactured a smile out of sheer will power and spoke swiftly, almost the first thing that came into her head. 'I was thinking about the winter months ahead. It's beautiful here now, but once I'm back in England, there'll be the bad months to come—rain and cold. I'm not looking forward to them one bit.'

'Live for the present,' he advised. 'I've found it pointless to bother about the future or the past—and as for the weather in England, I know about it. I had three winters in your country, but it isn't the only place where there's rain and cold. It can be very wet in this area, sometimes for weeks on end.'

'Were you ever in London?' asked Liz.

'Mmm, for a year, about four years ago. I was attending an agricultural college, specialising in animal husbandry together with a little veterinary work; I learned a lot. You come and learn to steer, it's not difficult.'

'Uh-uh,' Liz shook her head. 'The way you're twiddling that wheel, it looks very complicated.' She didn't want to be too close to him, not while his stepmother was asleep, and she had noticed he was very circumspect whenever Vivienne was near. She was near now, but from where Liz was sitting, she could see the Frenchwoman's eyes were closed.

'Scared?' he asked.

'Since you ask, yes!' Liz glared at him. 'I'm not looking for any more trouble. That's what you've come to mean for me—trouble! First a tree across my path. . . .'

'. . . And the sort of trouble I gave you up on the hill?' He raised an eyebrow and slanted a glinting, grey gaze at her.

'Precisely,' she agreed. 'That sort of thing I can do without. I told you once before, I'm very well adjusted. I'm a widow and I'm quite content as I am. I've no desire for any other relationship, and certainly not a tawdry holiday romance.'

'It could be more than that,' he murmured softly.

Liz's heart started pounding and she could feel the adrenalin starting to flow—All this and he wasn't even touching her! Warning bells sounded in her head and she looked round for something to do—an excuse to move away, but there was nothing. They were on their way back to Dieudonné, the boys, healthily tired, were up in the prow, quiet for once; nobody wanted anything to eat or drink, and if she walked away, it might look as though she was scared. The only thing to do was to stay put and brazen it out.

'An untawdry holiday romance?' She widened her smile. 'All moonlight and the scent of roses? A memory to keep me warm during the winter? No, thanks, Jean-Marc; save your energies for Marie-France and your other friends. I'm not in the market for trash.'

'And if I wasn't offering trash?'

Liz shrugged, not the graceful continental gesture but the less subtle, British variety; a brusque gesture that said 'I don't care'. She looked at him straightly. 'I've been offered consolation before, many times, and I'll tell you the same as I told them. I don't want it, I don't need it!'

'But you do.' He looked back at her and for a second she almost thought he was sincere. 'I think you *do* need it and badly—not consolation but loving. You haven't had any of that for a long time and you haven't been able to give any either.'

'Oh dear,' she sighed. 'I don't think anybody ever listens to what I say—you certainly don't. Save the psycho-analysis for somebody who appreciates it, please. In any case, you've got it all wrong.' She allowed the ice to creep back into her voice and her deep blue eyes became hard. 'You should know content when you see it, and that's what I am, contented. I like being the way I am, and I assure you, I intend to stay that way; no worries and no commitments.'

'Is all not well with Anglo-French relations?' Vivienne's soft voice interrupted their conversation. She gave a little silvery laugh as she left her seat in front of the wheel-house and came to stand by them. 'You two look as though you're quarrelling. Jean-Marc, shame on you! Where is your sense of hospitality? It isn't kind or even good manners to aggravate our guest.'

'No blame to Jean-Marc.' Liz eyed his stepmother warily. The last time she had looked at the Frenchwoman, she could have sworn Vivienne was asleep, and she wondered how long she had been awake and how much of the conversation she had heard. 'There's nothing wrong with international relations,' she smiled. 'We just haven't arrived at the Entente Cordiale stage yet.'

'But we're working towards it,' Jean-Marc added gravely.

# CHAPTER SEVEN

LIZ woke early to a still and silent house. Further sleep was impossible, so she slipped out of bed and into the shower, planning her morning. She didn't feel in the mood for company, certainly not to have to cope with Ham at breakfast time, so she would go off to the farm as soon as she was dressed and look at what progress had been made on her car. She would also dally over the inspection so that she arrived back too late for the communal breakfast—Berthe would always make her a cup of coffee; they were quite good friends now.

Silently she crept back from the bathroom to dress and tie back her hair. A layer of moisturiser sufficed for her face—after all, there would be nobody to see her unless the mechanic came early and he paid no attention to human beings unless they started making a noise as if they had a worn bearing.

There were one or two squeaky stairs which might cause somebody to wake if she trod on them, so she did what she had always wanted to do, slid down the curving sweep of the wide banister rail to land in the hall and scamper soft-footed to the door where she let herself out into the bright morning sunshine. Already it was quite warm, the dew had disappeared, the scent of roses was everywhere, and with a grunt of pleasure Liz started off on the walk down to the farm, revelling in the peace and quiet which would give her time to get her thoughts back into order.

She was intent on escape, not just because Avignon

and her memories lay at the end of her journey but because those memories were a defence between herself and the rest of the world. Behind it, she was safe, there was no emotionalism to tear at her, and safely behind it she didn't become involved with other people. Involvement brought pain, and of that she had suffered her share already. She wanted no more! Beneath the placid sunlit surface of Dieudonné, she sensed a danger lurking for her, a swift, dark tide that threatened her and her peace of mind. Already, she could feel her defences crumbling under the onslaught—and the reason stood out a mile.

That reason stood six foot in his stockinged feet, had black curly hair and was called Jean-Marc. What was worse, he was getting to her. Of course, it didn't mean anything, it was simply a matter of propinquity—she was a woman, he was a man, and a very attractive one, loaded with charisma and dangerous—he specialised in a subtle, slithery approach.

Liz flapped her hands to disperse a cloud of gnats which were circling her head and unconsciously squared her shoulders and lifted her chin, while her nostrils flared like a warhorse sensing battle. There was no reason, she told herself, for this odd feeling she was walking with danger, but try as she would, it refused to be shaken off. The feeling was there, it was walking beside her down this sunlit road and its cold breath made the hairs on the back of her neck prickle.

As if she was trying to outrun it, she broke into an easy lope, her long legs moving rhythmically to cover the distance and her sneakers stirring up puffs of dust with every step, so that when she turned in at the farmyard, she was breathing fast and there were trickles of perspiration down her back and between her breasts.

To cool down and recover her breath, she walked about, peering into the various sheds. The cows had been milked and now stood, head down in their stalls, their noses buried in mangers full of feed, tails swishing lazily over their satiny flanks.

A scrawny hen with one malignant eye squawked at her before resuming her industrious scratching and a thin, wild-looking cat raced past her, intent on its own business, but the animals were the only sign of life; the cowman and his helper must have gone home for breakfast.

Liz wandered into the shed used as a garage and in the gloom she could see the Mini Traveller, but not very well, so she pushed open the big doors of the shed to let in more light before she started her inspection. She nodded to herself contentedly; the car looked all right. All the bits were back on and although the front parts lacked the gloss of the finished article, it looked roadworthy, and that was the important thing. All that was necessary was that it should go!

'Not quite ready yet.' Jean-Marc had come up behind her silently and she whirled to face him.

'Don't creep!' she scolded. 'You could frighten me out of a year's growth doing that!'

'I hope not,' he grinned at her, his eyes sliding appreciatively over her long slenderness. 'You're delightful as you are, so don't grow any more.'

'The car——' she ignored both his appreciation and his closeness. 'I don't care what it looks like as long as it goes, and it looks as though it could go now. All it needs is that masking tape taken off—I'm not fussy about the paintwork. There'll be plenty of time to see to that when I get home.'

'Impatient,' he reproved her. 'What's the hurry to go?

Have we ill-treated you, or have you come out too early? It's before breakfast and it's made you bad-tempered. Come across to the house. I'll make you some coffee and you can tell me what you think of the *salon*, the bathroom, the downstairs cloakroom and all the other things which have been done since you were here last.'

It would be churlish to refuse, and the thought of hot fresh coffee was a lure which she couldn't resist, so she allowed herself to be steered across the sunlit yard.

'But couldn't the mechanic hurry up?' She looked up at him as she went. 'There can't be all that much left to do, and I want to be on my way.'

'You've been bored staying here?'

'Oh no,' she denied vigorously; boredom had been the least of her worries. 'Of course not. I've enjoyed most of it very much and it's been kind of you to have me—an unexpected, uninvited guest. It's just that. . . .' and her voice faded away into an indistinct mumble, utterly unlike her normally clear tones. She couldn't very well tell him she'd felt threatened ever since she'd arrived—he would ask who she thought was threatening her, and how could she say 'You are!' 'I'm bound for farther south,' she muttered defiantly.

'The grass is greener in Avignon?' Jean-Marc suggested without a smile.

'In actual fact, I know it isn't.' From the porch step, Liz looked at the view of tall trees and lush meadows which sloped down to the river. 'But metaphorically speaking, yes! The grass is greener there—besides, I like Roman France. . . .'

'. . . And it's where you went on your wedding journey. I know that—Ham let it slip, but don't blame him, he's only a boy. You sound like an old woman who has nothing to look forward to, who has only memories left. But you're not old, Liz, you're young— you should be looking forward, not over your shoulder.'

'That's enough.' She gave him a tight, mirthless smile. 'You're not saying anything new, you know; I've heard it all before—so many times from so many people, but with you I'm at a disadvantage. I can't tell you to shut up!'

'Why not, if that's the way you feel?' Jean-Marc raised an eyebrow while his eyes twinkled. 'Don't stand on ceremony with me, Liz; you didn't when you first arrived, remember? You had no hesitation in telling me to mind my own business, you damned me to hell, you scolded because you thought I'd been trifling with the affections of a teenage girl; I even believe you blamed me for allowing one of my trees to be blown across the drive so that you could run into it. Oh, yes, and I'm too harsh with young boys who don't tidy up after themselves, and I believe you think, although you've never said it, that I've the instincts of a lecher.'

Liz raised her chin and her nostrils thinned with temper. 'You're holding all that against me,' she snorted, fighting against the firm hand that impelled her into the farmhouse. 'O.K., so I was a bit upset at the time, I wasn't thinking straight and I said far more than I'd any right to, but you don't have to rub it in! I freely admit that on present performance, you're no more of a bully or a flirt than any other man of my acquaintance—and as for the lechery bit, I didn't ever actually *say* it. Most men seemed to be that way inclined anyway, so what's the odds?'

She adopted a demure look which held a hint of penitence. 'I did apologise at the time and I'll do it again—apologise, I mean. Not for thinking something about you which is probably true, though, but for saying it out loud!'

'Vixen!' he chuckled. 'Wait a moment while I work out just what you've said.' He frowned in concentration and then his eyebrows flew up again. 'Let's forget it, shall we? I've an idea you've made matters worse, not better.'

'You said you'd forget about it before,' said Liz in mock humility, 'but you didn't. Are you going to throw it in my face whenever I reject your advice?'

'It struck a spark,' he mused. 'For one moment, you became alive, but. . . .'

'. . . I'm alive all the time,' she interrupted fiercely. 'And now, can we get on, please? Where's this *salon* you're so proud of? Oh!' as he opened a door and pushed her inside. 'Now this is really something, it looks just like the adverts in the glossies—split level, dining area and *salon* combined—hide upholstery, that must have cost you a pretty packet, you didn't resurrect that from storage.' She spoke without thinking.

'I saw it, I liked it,' he admitted, 'and after that, nothing else would do. But you like the arrangement? There never was a dining room in this house, everybody always ate in the kitchen and it would have spoiled the outline to build one on.'

'It's a very good arrangement,' she commented as she walked around, trailing her fingers over polished wood, 'and I love the fireplace, it's not quite big enough to roast an ox, but if you found a very small one. . . .' Some of the tension was draining out of her, but she knew she still had to be careful. 'But don't pay too much attention to what I think,' she continued. 'I'm hardly an expert in this field. My only home since I left home is a tiny London flat, and you don't arrange furniture in it, you put it where you won't fall over it, the place is that small. You could put my kitchen in your porch and still have room for a big dog kennel. Not that I use it all that much.'

'You mean you can't cook?' Jean-Marc's lips twitched while his face took on a horrified expression.

'Oh,' she explained airily, 'I can grill the odd chop and fix a salad, but nobody could ever call me domesticated. I've had no training and very little experience.'

'Perhaps your talents lie in another direction?' He pulled her away from the well worn sideboard where she was playing with the brass handles. 'Come upstairs, things are looking better there as well.'

'You mentioned coffee,' she demurred.

'After you've seen upstairs,' and suddenly Liz felt unaccountably sorry for him, renovating this house for his own use and with nobody to give him a word of encouragement. She couldn't imagine his stepmother going into raptures about this little old house, not even if it was done out like a palace. Vivienne couldn't have liked it very much in the first place or she would never have persuaded her late husband to buy the other house. Whatever her beginnings, Louis' mother had a delicate air of aristocracy about her which would have been out of place here; she was much more at home in her mini-chateau.

'Upstairs it is, then, if that's the price I have to pay for a cup of coffee.' She turned reluctantly and preceded him. It would never do to let him think she pitied him. Either he would reject it out of hand or he'd try to make capital of it, so she would gush with a great deal of insincerity, making it plain she was bored stiff!

And gush she did in a brittle, artificial tone, all over the new bathroom with its pale green tiles and forest green suite—'Such a sensible colour when there's a young boy in the house who leaves everything in a mess.' That came out sweetly but poisonously before she peeped into what would be Louis' room, where she gushed some more over the sanded and newly waxed floorboards that glowed golden in between dark brown scatter rugs, the cupboards and shelving which would hold all a boy's possessions.

'You're overdoing it, Liz.' Jean-Marc spoke over her shoulder and she swung round to deny any such thing, but he laid a finger across her lips. 'A simple sentence complimenting me on my good taste would have been sufficient. Now come with me, I want to talk to you.' And he led her to his own door.

'And is the bed aired this time?' she asked acidly.

'No, it isn't,' he replied factually. 'It isn't even made up. The plastic cover's still on the mattress.' He swung the door open and Liz glanced briefly over her shoulder and quickly turned back to him. It was astounding how vulnerable she felt.

'Everything looks super.' She heard herself being stilted and over-enthusiastic and she flushed faintly. She shouldn't be like this, she wasn't a shy young girl. She was twenty-six and a widow, surely she had enough experience not to be embarrassed?

'I believe you're shy!' He examined her face with amusement. 'You're a very strange woman, Liz, or that's how you seem to me. I can think of at least half a dozen of your sex who could come in here without a trace of embarrassment.'

'It's the effect of the nasty experience I had last time I was here,' she snapped, while she pulled herself together and steadied her breathing. There didn't seem much she could do about her accelerated heartbeat. 'But it's a bit of a novelty to me, you see. Up until this holiday, I've denied myself the pleasure of inspecting men's bedrooms. Did you think perhaps that I made a habit of it?' She grimaced wryly. 'I'd soon have a wonderful reputation if that was the way I went on! It's hard enough to keep the wolves at bay and in their place as it is, never mind asking to see where they slept. They'd think I was measuring up, trying to see if there was room for two.'

'You have trouble with wolves?'

She nodded seriously. 'Sometimes, and that's an area where you could possibly help me. Tell me, and I'm asking because you ought to be able to give me a sensible answer—why is it that widows are looked on as fair game? Why is it that men don't realise that because a woman's had a husband, she hasn't turned into a nymphomaniac?'

'But I don't think you're a nymphomaniac,' he answered in an equally serious tone. 'To me, it's as though you've withdrawn from life, put yourself into cold store. Maybe that's what's the challenge—most men like to think they're capable of defrosting the most determined woman.'

'Typical male arrogance!' she glared at him.

'I think not,' he drawled, advancing on her, and Liz backed away until the bedrail caught at the back of her knees, halting any further retreat. 'You were defrosting very nicely up on the hill.'

'That was below the belt,' she scolded. 'You could say I was carried away by the sunshine, some pleasant company and a holiday atmosphere, or you could say I was taken in by an innocent approach—I was sneaked up on from behind. Usually I'm prepared for trouble, but I didn't think I'd have to defend myself from you. After all, I'm your guest, I wasn't expecting to have to fend off unwelcome advances from my host.'

'I handled you with kid gloves,' Jean-Marc protested. 'I had to. You're like a child who's had a painful burn, you're afraid of the fire. Learn, Liz—learn that love isn't always painful, that it doesn't always get cut off almost before it's begun.' He had advanced so far towards her that now, they were almost touching and with the bed at her back, Liz could retreat no further.

She clenched her hands at her sides and determined to be calm and dignified. Running away would be cowardly, and in any case, she couldn't get past him. He loomed there, big and broad, blocking her passage to freedom.

'In my own time,' she said coolly. 'I don't like being rushed. One day I expect I shall meet somebody, but that's looking a long way ahead.'

'Yes? Is that what you intend? To meet some man, some undemanding man who will be content with the little you'll give him, the half woman you'll still be—a man who won't mind not having all of you? You're asking to be hurt again if that's what you intend, because one day that man will wake up and realise what he's missing, and then you'll find yourself sharing him with another woman who can give him what you can't!'

Liz flushed with anger, momentarily forgetting her fear and embarrassment. 'That's a filthy thing to say!' she raged. 'And anyway, you've got it all wrong—but I'm not going to be polite any longer, you don't deserve it, not when you say things like that. I'm telling you now, mind your own business!'

'But I'm making it my business.' Jean-Marc remained

calm and undisturbed. His mouth curved into a smile
and his hands came hard on her shoulders, making her
flinch away from him. 'Stop trying to escape, Liz,
there's nowhere for you to run and nobody you can
hide behind. This is your moment of truth—you
remember I told you, if I saw something I wanted, I got
it, and nothing else would do.'

'You were speaking of household goods, I believe.'
She raised her nose in the air. 'Things you could buy in
a shop—you can't apply that to human beings, to
people who can think for themselves. And I hope you
don't mean that you want me, because if you do, you're
going to be disappointed! I've a mind of my own. I also
know what I want, and if you start using force, I'll
scream the place down!'

They were brave words, but all the time she was
saying them, her heart was beating madly and she was
shouting at herself. Why had she let this develop—she'd
surely had enough experience of avoiding sticky
situations. A light laugh, a jokey comment and it would
all have assumed the proportions of a rather gay and
far from serious flirtation. She could have handled that,
even a few meaningless kisses. What would they have
mattered?

'No force, *mignonne*, just a little friendly persuasion,
like this,' and his hands jerked her towards him so that
she came hard against his body with her mouth open on
a gasp of outrage and to yell defiance at him; and then
his mouth was on hers and the yell and gasp were
stifled.

'I don't force any woman,' Jean-Marc whispered
against her lips, and his arms tightened about her,
drawing her closer until she became aware of the
shrieking protest from each nerve from breast to thigh.

'No, don't look at me with those frightened eyes, *mignonne*. Close them, you've nothing to fear.'

His mouth found hers again, and gradually her protest died away in a flood of new excitement which uncoiled itself from her stomach in a wave of heat which crept along every nerve in her body so that she tingled all over. While she could still think, her mind went on assessing, but it wasn't a well thought out reasoning. It was a crazy jumble of thoughts and impressions, disconnected and fragmentary.

Was this the danger she had felt threatening her? This swift, dark, flowing tide which threatened to sweep her away from her steady, sensible life. She had done her best to avoid it and it was as if she'd never really tried— all her efforts had been in vain. Worse still, Jean-Marc knew exactly what he was doing to her, he was home and dry and he knew it! Liz could feel the confidence in his fingers as they probed at her swollen breast beneath the thin stuff of her shirt. She heard her own involuntary moan of pleasure—but this wasn't what *she* wanted, what she had known before. She and Bev had been in love, true love, bright and shiny with newness and yet as old as they were. The edges had been worn smooth by years of knowing each other, they didn't hurt each other, and that was what she wanted the second time around, if she ever decided to take that step again. Another man like Bev—a man with whom she'd be safe—be in control of herself, her emotions, her senses.

She didn't want this—this losing of her everything, even her own identity. She didn't want to be swept along on a tide of passion—depending on a man's hands, the sound of his voice, the touch of his mouth. The voice came to her ears now, whispering things huskily in his own language, and she was so far gone she could hardly understand a word—and then her nerve ends ceased their protest and she began to take pleasure in the touch of his hands against her skin.

His mouth left the warm hollow between her breasts and came back to demand against hers, and her hands weren't pushing him away any more. They were stroking his shoulders, her fingers tracing the lines of muscle and bone before they slid up to tangle with the crisp hair at the back of his head and she was holding him as closely as he held her.

She was flooded with a sweet warmth and could feel herself sliding into a soft darkness where her legs had lost the strength to hold her upright so that she sagged against him. The plastic wrappings squeaked and crackled as Jean-Marc lowered her on to the bed, and then he was beside her, drawing her back into his arms, and her soft mouth searched blindly for his because she couldn't bear to let a second slip away from her.

He raised his head to look down into her bemused eyes. 'Are you afraid I'll take advantage of you?' he asked softly, and when she looked at his face, his eyes were hooded as though he was afraid of her answer.

Liz fought for composure and from somewhere it came. She was able to raise quiet eyes to his and shake her head. 'No, I don't have any such inflated idea of my charms and I'm quite sure you wouldn't do anything I didn't want. I'm sure you're not the type of man who would get a kick out of beating down opposition or of forcing yourself where you're not wanted. It wouldn't make you feel good, because brute force doesn't appeal to you, does it?'

'True.' He raised himself on one elbow and looked down at her still flushed face. 'I prefer a more subtle approach—but as for beating down opposition. I don't think there would be very much, would there?' They were both talking in whispers as though there was somebody listening at the door. Jean-Marc stroked her cheek with a long finger, bringing it to touch her lower lip which was slightly swollen. 'I hurt you,' he murmured. 'Forgive me for that, *mignonne*, but I think we both needed this.'

'I didn't need it.' Liz controlled the sob which rose in her throat at his tenderness. 'Truly I didn't. I was quite happy as I was.'

'But you must learn, *ma mie*,' he said into the loose fronds of hair that curled about her forehead. 'The past may have been sweet, but the present and the future may be even sweeter; nobody can weep for ever. I can show you, prove to you that the future can be as good and warm as anything that's gone before,' The finger slipped under her chin, forcing her face to turn to him. 'But we'll play it your way, *ma petite*. I don't force any woman.'

Liz raised her eyes to his as though she was seeking the truth, and thought she heard him give a sigh of content as he pulled her closer and laid his cheek against hers. Suddenly she wanted to cry, to lay her head against his chest and howl like a hurt child. Why couldn't she accept what he was offering? It would all be so much easier that way—all very light and casual with no thought of tomorrow—but that wasn't the way she was made. It wouldn't be easy for her to go along with him, but he had demonstrated, pretty effectively, that he was quite capable of steering her up to the point where she would lose control.

'You could probably make me,' she admitted sadly. 'My morals seem to have vanished somewhere along the line, but I think I might be ashamed of myself afterwards and that would spoil it for both of us. I don't think I'm much good at casual relationships.'

'*Mignonne*,' it was no more than a husky whisper as his lips touched each of her eyelids in turn, 'you don't. . . .'

Whatever he intended to say was lost in the roar of a tractor entering the yard, followed by the heavy trundle of a much bigger vehicle. There was a shouting and calling of men's voices, and Jean-Marc gave his customary shrug as he struggled to his feet and walked across to the window, tucking his shirt back inside his trousers as he went.

'The co-op lorry to collect the milk. The men are there, ours with them, so our interlude of peace is over. The world has intruded on us, but it's not fatal. We'll continue this later when I can be sure we'll have no interruptions.' His eyes flicked to where Liz was trying to restore a little order to her rumpled appearance and he smiled. 'I'll take you back to the house straight away. Berthe makes much better coffee than either of us and she'll be waiting for us.'

'It's a good job the world did intrude,' she said severely as she walked along the road beside him. 'We—that is—it was all becoming too serious for words.'

'Exactly,' he slanted a smile down at her. 'We'd reached the point where words were no longer enough—where action was necessary, and I have to talk to you before that.'

'There's nothing really to talk about,' she said. 'You made a pass at me,' she continued as though she was thinking aloud, 'you made a pass, I declined, end of story—so we'll move on to something else. What shall you call your farmhouse now?' It was a safe subject and she elaborated. 'When you move into it, I mean, and what are you going to do with Dieudonné?'

'I shall take the name with me.' He was serious, it was a matter dear to him. 'It came from the farm, so it's only fair it should go back there. The St Clairs and Dieudonné have meant the same thing in these parts for a long time. As for the other house, what do you suggest? It could be let, sold or turned into *gites* for visitors.'

'Well,' Liz wrinkled her brow, 'if you're not going to live in it, you'll have to do something. If it stays empty, it'll deteriorate. Maybe you'll find somebody frightfully wealthy who appreciates all that elegance and they'll buy it from you—or you could open it up and charge tourists an admission fee.'

'Too much competition,' he smiled lazily. 'People come to the Loire valley to see the grand chateaux, not little copies. But as you say, it can't be left empty. I think it must be sold. If it was let, I would still be responsible for major repairs, or it could be renamed Chateau de Villiers and let to foreign visitors during the summer months. I'll have a word with the Tourist Bureau about it. If they don't want it and it can't be sold, I shall pull it down.'

'That's rather extreme, isn't it?'

'But practical, Liz.' He scowled into the sun, his black eyebrows in a straight line above his eyes. 'Think of this place as a business—the farm, the vineyard. It has to be run at a profit and we can't afford to spend money on a white elephant when we need it for fertilisers, new machinery and breeding stock. Do you like the house so much?'

'N-no.' She scuffed her feet, kicking up clouds of

white dust as she walked. 'It's very nice to look at but I wouldn't want to live in it but it seems a shame to tear it down.'

'Pure sentimentality,' he snorted, 'and I thought you were a practical young woman! You've disappointed me.'

They were nearing the gates and Liz wanted to be done with the subject—it had nothing to do with her and she didn't want to become involved or to waste time discussing it. She wanted to get away somewhere on her own, somewhere private where she could indulge in a bit of deep thinking.

'Then it's up to you. Heavens!' she glanced briefly at her watch. 'No wonder I'm hungry and thirsty, it's nearly nine o'clock! Berthe will have given us up for lost,' and she took to her heels and fled up the driveway.

While she washed and tidied herself for breakfast, she tried to decide what was to be done; she even tried to be honest with herself. It's a typical holiday romance, she reminded herself. Very glamorous, a bit torrid— everybody has one at some time or another. They don't last! At last, satisfied with her appearance, she ran lightly down the stairs and walked sedately along the passageway to the kitchen. Berthe wasn't there, but Jean-Marc waved the coffee pot at her and at her nod, filled her cup. Liz picked it up and with a croissant in her other hand, she walked across to the kitchen window and looked out over the gardens at the back of the house. She felt rather than heard him come to stand behind her.

'Liz?' His hand was on her shoulder, gently pulling her back to rest against him, but she stiffened her body. 'You're very beautiful.' It came as a whisper in her ear.

'That's hardly a novel approach,' she said hardily without turning her head from her contemplation of the flower beds. 'I think I prefer the one where the man says he loves me for the quality of my mind.'

As a brush-off, it was good and it worked. She felt him withdraw, but instead of triumph she only felt cold and lonely.

# CHAPTER EIGHT

SINCE the boys had only the afternoon to spend and no hope of any other transport save the bus they both agreed that Blois was out of reach, but they riffled through the guides and came up with a second choice. The chateau of Le Plessis-Bourré was only an hour's journey, if that, and the day needn't be wasted. Liz breathed a sigh of relief when Vivienne declined to go and Jean-Marc said he had things to do which would occupy him until dinner time.

This meant Liz would have the afternoon to herself she didn't count the boys as company and she firmly rejected Jean-Marc's offer to either the Matra or the small Fiat.

'We'll go by bus,' she said definitely. 'I'd be asking for another accident in a strange car, and if I'm going to have an accident, I'd prefer to have it in my own car and with no children about.' She became gloomy. 'I think I've lost my nerve.'

Vivienne nodded wisely. 'It often happens. The best thing after an accident is to start driving straight away.'

'Which is very easy to say,' Liz controlled her irritation but even so, she sounded snappish, 'but I didn't have the chance. However, we'll take the bus from Villiers, which will be much safer. I'd never be able to hold my head up again if somebody had to be called out to rescue another dead car and two or three broken bodies!'

But it wasn't only the thought of driving a strange

car that made her feel uneasy; she had been feeling definitely strained ever since the boys had come back from the swimming pool. She and Jean-Marc had been on the drive waiting for them when they had come sweeping in, letting their bicycles drop where they dismounted and scattering wet towels and trunks in all directions as they rushed up. This time, Jean-Marc didn't seem to mind the mess.

'So much enthusiasm!' he had smiled at her, and she had found herself smiling back as she quoted, '. . . and only one overworked, middle-aged woman to clear up after them!' as she rescued the towels from being trampled on. And then, in the heat of the day, everything went cold for her and she was left feeling that something bitter and inimical had reached out to touch her, sending a icy prickle down her back despite the warm breeze.

Ham and Louis had flung themselves face down on the lawn, arms and legs flapping as they demonstrated a new stroke they had been learning. Their voices had been loudly recounting the details of their performance, but instead of laughing at them, as Jean-Marc was doing, Liz had felt that chill so that she turned swiftly to find Vivienne directly behind her, with a speculative look in her large dark eyes and her mouth a tight line.

'Get off the grass,' she scolded Louis in French. 'You'll spoil it. These lawns weren't turfed for you to walk on! Jean-Marc,' she turned to him, 'is that your idea of discipline? Me, I think you're letting my son become badly behaved. He must learn not to spoil things, and if you encourage him, I shall have to do something about it. I've been through the house this morning and found scratches on the furniture, chipped and cracked plates. . . .'

Liz didn't wait for any more, she muttered 'Race you to the house', and at Ham's nod, they set off. Louis was quick to catch on, he was abreast of them before they'd taken ten paces. Liz waited for the boys to wash and tidy themselves, and then all three of them walked sedately down to lunch. It was obvious to her that Vivienne hated noise, damage and untidiness, and perhaps it was anger at that which had been responsible for the feeling of unease which had afflicted Liz, but she didn't think so. There had been a malignancy about Vivienne, and surely a few scratches, some chipped plates and a romp on the lawn weren't enough to rouse an emotion as violent as that?

Liz had never considered herself a particularly imaginative person, and she became angry with herself for being upset by something she had only felt and thought she had seen, but, sitting at the lunch table, sandwiched between the boys and with Jean-Marc and with Vivienne facing them, she still felt tendrils of that unease coiled deep in her stomach. And as Vivienne spoke, the tendrils uncoiled so that the unease grew.

'You're still playing with that old farmhouse, Jean-Marc?' Louis' mother made a small, exasperated sound, and speaking as one would speak to a child who was wasting time, 'Isn't it time you stopped this nonsense? you've been working there yourself and you've had a man from the farm there, helping you for nearly a year, and all the time it's costing you money you can ill afford. How much longer are you going to continue with this nonsense?' Vivienne was speaking in French, as usual, and a light dawned on Liz; Louis' mother was unaware that Liz both spoke and understood French, and this was her way of conducting a private conversation—all very uncomfortable, and Liz shifted in her seat.

'A few months only,' Jean-Marc sounded serene and content. 'Actually, Louis and I could move down there the first week in September, but I think November would be a more convenient time.' He answered Vivienne in the same language, giving Liz a flick of his grey eyes which seemed to hold a warning light.

'So long a delay?' his stepmother laughed, a tinkly, aggravating sound—so aggravating that Liz bit her lip hard. 'Berthe told me the place was almost ready, so what are you waiting for, *my* permission?'

'Is that necessary?' He looked at his stepmother and she coloured slightly under his gaze. 'No,' he smiled, and it wasn't anything like the smile Liz had seen on his face, it was tight, hard and there was little mirth in it. 'No, it isn't, madame, not necessary at all. I have other reasons, quite simple ones. September is going to be a busy month for the wine co-operative, there's the grape harvest to get in and Dieudonné must do its share, and in October I intend to do a lot of winter ploughing and overhaul the machinery. . . .'

'Bucolic activity!' Vivienne looked down her nose and made a moue of distaste as though she'd just smelled fertilizer. 'Tell me, Jean-Marc, do you intend to turn my son into a country boy with not a thought in his head but filthy farm work and fields of crops?'

'It's a good healthy life,' there were white patches of anger at the sides of his nose, 'and with modern methods and machinery, a lot of the hard work has vanished. Today, farming is like any other profession, not dirty at all. Besides, Louis is a farmer's son, it's in his blood. . . .'

'He is also intelligent,' Vivienne interrupted angrily, snapping the words out like a spitting cat.

'Then he'll make an intelligent farmer.' Jean-Marc

kept his eyes on his plate, but the knuckles of the hand which held his fork were white.

'And me?' Vivienne was icy with disapproval. 'When I come to see my son, what about me? Shall I be expected to stay in that little house with all the smells of the farmyard under my nose?'

'Of course, *madame*.' He sounded quite unconcerned, although there was the jerk of a small muscle along the side of his jaw as though he was controlling himself with difficulty; although whether it was laughter or rage he was suppressing wasn't obvious. 'It should be no hardship for you to visit the farm for a couple of days.'

'Then my visits will be infrequent—so infrequent I think I shall take Louis back to Paris with me.' Vivienne leaned back in her chair—her eyes were no longer soft and liquid, they had become hard and sparkled with something like malice. 'This isn't the life I want for my son. Your crops and manure will dull the fine edges of his mind, he will become a peasant.'

Liz felt the slight, small figure beside her stiffen and she gave Louis a swift, unobtrusive smile. He went on eating his lunch, but she noticed his eyes—all the merriment had gone and they were deep pools of misery.

'Impossible, *madame*,' Jean-Marc said firmly, and Liz thought she could see the child relaxing a little. 'Impossible that he will become a peasant and also impossible that you should take him back to Paris. I would never permit that and you know it—and we'll not quarrel about it now, if you please; it would upset my brother.'

'And my house?' Vivienne went on to another tack. 'What do you intend to do with that?'

'Let it, sell it or pull it down,' he answered

reasonably. 'And this is a private matter which should be discussed privately, if there's any need for discussion. Myself, I see no need at all. Louis will stay here, we shall move down to the farm and this house and its contents will be disposed of. You, of course, may do whatever you wish.'

He ended on a note of such finality that nobody spoke for the rest of the meal, and Liz sat through it, wishing she'd never left England, never become involved with this family. She had tried to shut her ears, but it had been quite impossible. Together with a distaste for hearing other people's affairs discussed, she was filled with a rage which was fast growing into an outsized irritation. It wasn't right, she scolded silently, for a child to be made a bone of contention, especially not a sensitive little boy like Louis, and she glared under her lashes at Jean-Marc and Vivienne. To use the boy in some sort of private war—how dared they! A lot of little things she had noticed now slotted into place— the way Jean-Marc rarely talked to his stepmother and never talked about her—when she was out of sight, he behaved as though she didn't exist!

And Vivienne—an unnatural mother if she ever saw one; Liz remembered when Louis had stumbled against her in the boat, dirtying her clothes—she could never recall her own mother, or Marcie for that matter, ever behaving like that. In fact, Marcie had often forgone buying a suit or a dress she liked because it wouldn't stand up to an assault from Ham's sticky fingers!

Anyway, if Jean-Marc and Vivienne wanted to squabble over the boy, they should do it when he was absent or out of earshot, and it wasn't right that either of them should use him as a lever to get what they wanted. It was the most outrageous form of blackmail and very bad for Louis. Liz would have liked to bang both their heads together and tell them to save their nastiness for another time when the boy couldn't hear them.

She moved her chair slightly and let her hand rest in Louis' where it was clenched on his knee. She wouldn't have dared make such a gesture to Ham; her nephew's ferocious dignity wouldn't let him accept comfort from a woman, but Louis wasn't Ham, he was much less robust, both physically and mentally. Liz was a little relieved as she felt the clenched fingers relax under her own, but her heart ached when he turned to look at her with eyes which were too old for his years, too full of adult knowledge for his young face.

Vivienne was now silent, although her face wore a mulish look that didn't augur well for future family relationships, and to break away from this deplorable meal, Liz glanced at her watch and squeaked with alarm.

'We'll have to be leaving soon,' she kept it chatty. 'Le Plessis-Bourré beckons and the bus won't wait. May we be excused?' and she hurried the boys from the table and out of the room at the speed of light.

They cycled down to Villiers in glum silence, stacked the bikes behind the swimming pool, where Louis said they would be perfectly safe, and caught the bus by the skin of their teeth. Le Plessis-Bourré was a pleasant little place and not in the grand manner—Liz sat on the grass outside while the boys went through it, closing her eyes and resting against a convenient small tree while she mentally rehearsed what she would say if she ever had the opportunity to give Jean-Marc and his stepmother a piece of her mind. It took quite a while, there was so much she would have liked to tell them, and she was only halfway through when Ham came blaring in her ear.

'I didn't understand a thing!' He sounded aggrieved. 'And we only brought Louis' book and that's all in French, so why can't *he* understand it?' Liz stretched out a hand and Ham put the offending book into it. The description of the cheateau occupied less then twenty lines and when she had skimmed through it, she understood little more than before.

'It's been written by one of those experts,' she snorted. 'All technical terms, and I don't know them, hardly anybody would—All I can tell you about it is that it says here, it was more "comfortable" to live in, but that's a lot of rot. It doesn't look comfortable to me! Sit down and have a drink, Berthe's put in some cans of Fanta.' Her antennae were bristling again; there was something different about the boys and Ham had an air of suppressed excitement which nearly always meant trouble, a trouble which was better scotched before it got under way.

'What's going on between you two?' she asked the question in a throwaway tone as if it had very little importance.

Louis raised his eyes from his can of drink and sidled nearer to her. 'I do not wish to go to Paris, Madame Liz.'

'That's right,' Ham was sturdy about it. 'Louis doesn't like it in Paris.'

'And you've decided to do something about it, I suppose,' Liz sighed with reluctant sympathy—she knew Ham very well; he liked organising things. 'You'd better tell me and we'll talk about it, see if it's practical.'

'Mmm,' Ham agreed casually. 'Louis says he's going to run away and hide till we go back to England, then we'll pick him up in the car and take him with us. That's quite a good idea, don't you think, and Mum won't mind, not when I tell her how. . . .'

'Bad planning.' Liz kept a straight face. 'We shan't be going back for two weeks, that's quite a long time, and Jean-Marc will find him in that time. Where were you thinking of hiding him, in the potting shed?'

'There isn't one,' Ham said gloomily—potting sheds were his favourite hideout. 'But,' he brightened, 'there's no need for him to hide away that long, not really, only till his mum goes back to Paris—then he can come out. He's got all the stuff, you know, and we thought the big barn would be just the place. He has a sleeping bag and a lantern that runs on batteries and I could take him down food and things. . . .'

'No!' Liz shook her head definitely. 'And don't look at me like that, as though I've disappointed you. You'd both be found out very quickly and then what would happen? You, Ham, would be sent home in disgrace and probably Louis wouldn't be able to come. . . .'

'. . . Mum's invited him for Christmas,' her nephew interrupted. 'It's all in the letter from her I had this morning. I showed it to Jean-Marc and he said Louis could come. . . .'

'He'll change his mind if you do anything stupid,' Liz said forcefully. 'Honestly, Ham, I'm not trying to put a spoke in your wheel or spoil things for you, but that sort of caper never works, and sometimes it can have nasty repercussions.'

'But if Louis' mum drags him back to Paris, I'll have to go home anyway,' Ham's logic was incontrovertible. 'I can't stay here on my own and I don't want to go to Paris. Louis says it's awful, all full of museums and things.'

Liz sighed. There wasn't much she could say, but what she said, she said with as much authority as she could dredge up. 'I'm sure Jean-Marc won't allow Louis to go to Paris.'

'It's because he doesn't have a wife.' Ham was sulky with disappointment. 'He's Louis' guardian, but it would be much better if he was married, then he'd have somebody to look after them properly and Louis' mum wouldn't be able to say he wasn't being taken care of.'

'Not our business!' Liz said sternly. 'I was going to say that if Louis does go to Paris, you can always come on with me.'

'But that's not having a holiday with Louis,' Ham was muttering defiantly. 'I shan't have anybody to talk to!'

'Maybe so,' Liz's sympathy was evaporating fast, 'but I want your promise, both of you, that you won't do anything stupid which'll make matters worse than they are now. Ham, if you show you can't behave sensibly then Louis' mum will be quite justified in taking him away from here. She'll say you're a bad influence.'

Ham wasn't convinced; it was reasonable, but it wasn't romantic enough. 'Louis says if he goes to Paris, he *will* run away. He's got lots of money, you know, he keeps a five-hundred-franc note pinned inside his jacket, and he's hidden his passport, the one he had last year when he went to Greece on a school trip. He says he'll come to England and nobody will think of looking for him there because they all think he can't speak enough English.'

Liz gasped and reached for the smaller boy, putting her arm round his shoulders. 'No, Louis,' she implored, using French because it was easier for him to understand. 'You mustn't ever run away from things, sooner or later you have to face up to them, so it's only a delaying action.'

'You don't run away, Madame Liz?' His dark eyes looked at her full of an age-old wisdom. 'But when you said you must go and I couldn't understand because it's much better here than in Avignon, Jean-Marc said you were running away.'

'Running away?' Liz snorted. 'What would I be running away from?'

'That's what I asked,' Louis nodded with wisdom, 'and Jean-Marc said you were running away from life, which seems very stupid to me, because it's with you all the time.'

Out of the mouths of babes and sucklings—Liz thought about it while she gathered up the empty cans to stuff in her bag, and she was still thinking about it when they were on the bus going back to Villiers. She sat in the seat in front of the boys, and although she kept her eyes firmly on the window, she saw nothing of the scenery jolting past. She wasn't running from life, she had simply withdrawn from it a little to nurse her memories—to have a breathing space while she got over the shock of her loss.

It didn't hurt quite so much now and she had stopped envying people who hadn't suffered as she had, but she was still wary of coping with other human beings—that was evident from her spineless behaviour since she'd arrived at Dieudonné! Her normal self would never have allowed Jean-Marc to take liberties in the first instance, and then there would have been no follow-up and her normal self, also, would never have wanted those liberties, not as her present unbalanced self did.

Perhaps she could find the sort of love she had had

with Bev, or something like it. It would mean going out and looking for it, not sitting at home, wallowing in grief and loss. Bev had always hated misery.

Liz thought some more. The past was dead and Bev with it, but it had helped shape her as she was now. She had better put it away, not to forget it completely but put it in a box, something tender and fragile to be put aside with a sprig of lavender, and as the bus drew into Villiers she counted up her memories—one earring, some photographs and Bev's watch.

With steady fingers, she began to undo the lizardskin strap about her wrist.

'Your mother is dining with friends in Angers tonight,' Jean-Marc said to Louis, and the sigh of relief which emanated from both boys was nearly strong enough to blow out all the candles in the elaborate candelabrum on the table. Liz raised her head when he spoke, her eyes widening. There was such a difference in his voice. Gone was his lazy good humour, the faint slurring of consonants; now it was all tight and harsh, and his face—she peeped at it from under her lashes— that was different as well.

It was as if all the humour and life had been drained from it, to leave a mask. He looked now as he had done the first time she had seen him, careless, reckless and bitter—the face of the fallen angel, as though he had fought with the devil and lost. Liz found herself wondering what hell he had been through this afternoon while she and the boys had been enjoying themselves.

However, she managed a pleasant, uncomplicated smile as he steered her from dining room to *salon* and she steered the conversation into what she thought was a safe channel.

'Louis took the wrong guide book, a French one, and I was mortified! I couldn't make head or tail of it. A great disappointment for Ham, and I'm afraid I've gone down several feet in his estimation. Perhaps you could do the honours for me when I'm gone.'

'You still intend to go?'

'Mmm, as soon as the car's ready.' That was the easy part—now for something a little more difficult. 'Er—if Louis accompanies his mother back to Paris. . . .' Her calm tones faltered a little as she felt a wave of pure rage sweep out from him to encompass her, but she caught herself up and continued smoothly enough. 'We discussed it this afternoon, what we would do, and I think it would be sensible, in that event, to take Ham on with me.'

'You discussed this with the boys?' Jean-Marc leaned forward towards her and instinctively she flinched, but the hand he had raised only fell on her shoulder, although his fingers tightened until she could feel them against the bones. There would be bruises tomorrow.

'Not so much me discussing it with them but them discussing it with me.' She fought for serenity. 'I hadn't realised things were so involved.'

'I see.' Abruptly, her shoulder was free and he walked over to the sideboard where he fiddled about and then came back to thrust a glass of something under her nose. 'Drink that,' he commanded. 'You look as though you need it, and we have to talk.'

'Thanks!' Liz replied dryly. Her new self, the forward-looking one which had come into being only that afternoon, was taking over and being almost nonchalant. She suspected the new self wasn't ready for close encounters yet, but there would be no harm in giving it some practice at word games.

'You shouldn't have spoken of that thing to the boys.' He flung himself into a chair opposite and let his head fall back almost wearily. 'I blame you for that.'

'You can thank me instead,' she muttered fiercely. 'Heaven alone knows what they might have got up to if I hadn't talked to them! In any case, they brought it up, not me.' As her breathing steadied, her flow of words increased and, with them, her confidence. 'And don't talk to me about blame! Any blame you can think of you should be carrying yourself, you and his mother. You did everything but fight over possession of him right under his nose—don't either of you know anything about child psychology? Louis was all set to scarper!'

'Scarper?' His eyebrows drew together in a frown. 'I'm sorry, but that's a new word for me. What does it mean?'

'Run away,' she said tersely. Already, she thought she'd said far more than she should, and she tried to keep the rest light, almost humorous. 'I suppose you could blame Ham for that; he has a terrific imagination and very little practicality to go with it. He's also possessed of a protective instinct for smaller kids and he's a bit of a romantic at heart.'

'No, Liz,' Jean-Marc looked across at her with the 'fallen angel' expression grooved deep on his handsome features, 'I shan't blame Ham. Louis has done this before—run away, I mean. Once he had half the police in Paris looking for him when he "scarpered", as you call it. He was only seven and a bit at the time, but he managed to get himself from Paris to this place without telling anybody what he meant to do. Ham might have been a helpful factor this time, but he certainly isn't responsible for my brother's plan to run away.'

'Big of you to admit it.' She was getting better at words games and she answered him tartly. 'Louis is insecure, he needs somebody to make it plain to him that he's not like a piece on a chessboard to be moved about from square to square whether he likes it or not.'

Jean-Marc unfolded himself from his chair and came to stand over her, his hands one on either side of her chair so that she was pinioned in it.

'You sound very interested in my brother, Liz, but I wonder how genuine you are. It's easy to tell other people what they should do, but would you be willing to do something about it yourself? You could give him security, you know, easily enough. Stay here, marry me!' He said it so calmly, so coolly that at first Liz thought she had misheard him. Then it sank in, and she squeaked.'

'M-m-marry!' She made to stand up, couldn't, and slumped back in the chair. 'You can't be serious! A couple of weeks' acquaintance—why, we're practically strangers! Oh, I see what it is,' and she thought she did. 'This is your way of telling me, in the nicest possible fashion, that I'm an interfering bitch, that none of it's any business of mine—and I agree with you wholeheartedly. I also apologise for sticking my nose in where it's not wanted—I shall leave tomorrow, and thank you for your hospitality!'

'Don't be a fool, Liz, I didn't mean it that way. I don't think you're interfering and you can "stick your nose" anywhere you wish—I don't think I like that expression, though.' He stood watching her face closely, and for a moment or so, the house was quiet about them with only the crackle and hiss of the log fire to break the silence. 'You—er—turn me down, then? You say you didn't enjoy what we had this morning?'

Liz gulped; she felt shame but she didn't let it show. This was her new self, and that self was going to be honest with him.

'As far as it went, yes, I did enjoy it, but I don't think I'd have wanted it to go any further. Please let me get out of this chair, I'm rather tired and I'd like to go to my room, if you please.' She looked pointedly at his long legs and the bulk of his body which was planted in front of her and denied her exit.

Almost at once he stood back from her, her way was clear, but as she rose, he moved in on her and his arms were about her. She looked up at him and saw the lines of strain gone from his face; the old expression, the one she knew so well was back, half humorous, half mockingly rueful.

'If we hadn't been interrupted, we'd have gone much further,' he murmured, 'and we'd have agreed about our relationship by now.'

'Then we should be grateful for the interruption. . . .'

'. . . Don't hope for one now, Liz.' He pulled her closer and she could feel the hard warmth of his body against hers from breast to thigh. 'We won't have one, you know. The boys are at the far end of the house and Louis' mother won't be back until dawn. No,' as she started to wriggle free, 'I'm not going to haul you off to my bed or ask to share yours. All I want is a little time with you—we'll make a little love, talk about the future. . . .'

'Please,' she put her hands on his chest and pushed against him, 'I told you this morning, I don't want to go even that far—and as for that insane proposal you've just made, I'm not ready for anything like that, not yet. You've done one good thing for me, I'll grant you that, I'm beginning to find my feet and rely on myself for the first time in years. You see, I've never had anything much to do with decision-making and I don't know if I'm up to it yet. If you're of the same mind in, say, a year's time, ask me then—but don't quote Louis' welfare as your motive, please. I wouldn't commit my life for that sort of reason.'

'I could make you change your mind.' There was a wry humour in his half threat and Liz eyed him stonily.

'I expect you could.' Suddenly she was very tired, almost too tired to cope. It would be so easy to let go, relax against him, leave all the decisions to him as she had always left them to her parents, to Bev, but something stopped her; it also made her snappish. 'You've had a hell of a lot of experience and I've had very little,' she pointed out. 'But I don't think the change would have anything to do with my mind! I'd probably give way to you, I think I'd want to, but. . . .'

'. . . you don't trust your instincts?

'No,' she shook her head sadly. 'I daren't, not about giving myself. My reasons, they'd have to be overwhelming and quite personal—purely physical satisfaction wouldn't be enough.'

'And I thought the English had lost much of their renowned coldness,' murmured Jean-Marc. 'Is that how it would be? You'd think about making love, whether it was the right time of day or night, whether you *felt* like it, whether it would make you late for an appointment at the hairdressers. The English are cold.'

Liz shrugged. 'Perhaps they are, I wouldn't know but I'm not speaking about a nation en bloc, I'm speaking about me.' She glanced at his mouth which was so close, she could see the pores of his skin and then she looked down at his arms which were holding her. She moved sightly and became wonderfully aware of the hardness of his thigh against hers, of the strength of his fingers as they stroked her back. A little shiver of something, it could have been excitement or despair, ran down her spine and difficult tears filled her eyes.

'Let me go, Jean-Marc,' she whispered. 'Please don't make me do something I might regret.'

'Could I?'

Her breasts ached as she stirred in his close embrace. 'Yes, you know you could, and I know it as well. That's why I'm asking for mercy.'

She felt his lips on her hair, on her brow and then on her eyelids before he raised his head. 'Go in peace, *mignonne*,' and his arms loosened their hold on her and she was free.

# CHAPTER NINE

In her bedroom, Liz halted, out of breath and with her heart hammering like a jungle tom-tom. The 'thinking' part of her was aglow with satisfaction, but the 'feeling' part was sobbing with frustration and her satisfied mind meant very little in comparison with her body, which was screaming with pain. But it would pass, it *had* to pass, or she would go mad with the ache that spread through every part of her.

It shouldn't be like this, she groaned aloud as she slid into bed—it had never been like this before and she was ashamed of it happening now. It brought her down to a level of need she had never known, never wanted to know—it diminished her, this screaming need to cease to be herself, to want only to become part of Jean-Marc.

In the darkness, she lay awake castigating herself but all the time knowing that if he came to her, tried the door and came in, she would accept anything he offered and there would have been no strings. 'Fool, fool, *fool*!' she almost shouted it aloud, so filled was she with a bitter rage at her own weakness.

'Liz, *Liz*!' The shouting wakened her and she stirred lethargically. It had been past dawn when she had fallen asleep and now it was—she glanced at her naked wrist—it was fairly late, she decided, seeing the patterns of sunlight that the louvred shutters spread across the floor and walls.

'What is it?' she snarled badtemperedly—oh lord, she

felt ghastly! She probably looked as awful as she felt, but it was Ham's shout that had wakened her and he wouldn't notice—she hoped!

He pushed the door and put his head round through the opening to look at her accusingly. 'Aren't you up yet?' he demanded.

'Does it look like it?' Liz's snarl turned into a grumble. 'What's the matter, is the house on fire?'

' 'Course not, silly,' Ham snorted. 'But we've all had breakfast, there's only you to come—and guess what, you don't know because you've been asleep, but everything's all right now. Jean-Marc came to see Louis and me last night after you'd gone to bed—we were still awake, talking and making plans, you know, and he said Louis was staying here.' While he had been talking, he had come further and further into the room until he was standing looking down on her. 'He said he wouldn't allow him to be taken off to Paris, which is a pity in one way because we'd worked out a splendid scheme, much better than the other one.'

'Heaven defended me from your schemes!' groaned Liz, and put a hand across her eyes to shield them from a stray bar of sunlight.

'And,' Ham was important, the bearer of news, 'Louis' mum is going back today, she's had her car brought round from the garage. It's a Porsche, a red one—just fancy her hiding it away like that. I'd have liked a ride in a Porsche,' he added plaintively.

Liz's memory stirred. How emotions could play havoc with one's senses! Now she remembered that red Porsche distinctly; it had been on the drive when she'd run back from the hill, but she'd been so upset, it hadn't registered.

'I expect Louis' mum has more respect for her

upholstery and paintwork to let you anywhere near it, you little hooligan.' Liz rolled over on her face. 'Go away and be bright and gladsome somewhere else, will you? I'm going to get up. Ask Berthe to give me ten minutes, I promise not to be any later.'

'I'll bring you a cup of coffee if you like,' he offered. 'What do you want with it?'

'Solitude!' She managed a grin while she felt like death. 'Don't bother though, I'll be down shortly; now, scat!'

When Ham had gone, she dragged herself to the bathroom and after a hasty shower, returned to the dressing table to set grimly about her face—not to enhance her good looks but to cover the ravages of a sleepless night. Moisturiser, foundation—two layers—blusher, lipstick and powder—she went through the routine as swiftly as possible, then brushed her hair until it looked less lank and screwed it up into the usual ponytail which she secured with a rubber band.

Berthe's good plain food seemed to have made a difference; Liz gazed down at her reflection with distaste; these jeans, the pair she travelled down in and hadn't worn since were almost indecent, they'd become so tight, but they would have to do, and thrusting her feet into a pair of flat sandals, she set off downstairs—to be surprised when she found Vivienne waiting at the bottom, ready dressed for the road.

Liz, aware of the contrast between Vivienne's well cut black silk crêpe and her own figure-hugging, well washed jeans topped with an Indian cotton drip-dry shirt bought cheaply from a market stall, felt rather like an underprivileged member of an ethnic minority, but she summoned up a smile and murmured about being late for breakfast in an apologetic tone.

'Yes, I suppose you are.' Vivienne consulted her small, delicate-looking watch. 'Come into the *salon*, I'll have Berthe bring you something there. I'm returning to Paris this morning and I think we should have a talk before I go. No,' as Liz began to open her mouth, 'I insist. After all, we don't know each other very well, do we? Even after we've been in the same house for several days. Come,' and a small hand was tucked under Liz's elbow to steer her gently but firmly away from the kitchen regions and into the dining room.

'We used always to have breakfast here in the dining room, so much more elegant,' Vivienne smiled. 'We could talk, discuss the events of the day which had passed and plan for tomorrow, but in front of Berthe, that's impossible. People living in small communities gossip so, don't you find?'

'I've never lived in one—a small community, I mean.' Liz settled into her usual chair and watched as Vivienne tugged gracefully at a bell pull. There was no fire in here this morning, the ashes of last night's had been cleared away and everything was shining—the over-worked, middle-aged woman, she supposed, and of whom she had only caught the occasional glimpse. Even the flowers had been changed, and the room was full of the heavy perfume from a bowl of velvety dark red roses.

'Ah,' Vivienne looked understanding. 'But me, I was brought up, not in a small community but in a very close one. My father was in Government service, a responsible post, you understand, and friends and servants had to be chosen with care.'

'Umm,' Liz tried not to be bored. 'Ham, my nephew, tells me you're leaving for Paris today. I've often wondered if living in Paris is anything like living in London.' As an effort to change the subject of the conversation, it failed. Louis' mother was in a 'Dieudonné'-orientated frame of mind and she was not going to talk about life in Paris.

'You look a little distraite this morning, Liz—I hope our Jean-Marc has not been at his usual tricks?'

'Usual tricks?' Liz pretended nicely to surprise. Somehow she knew this had been coming, it didn't surprise her in the least, it was all part of the dark current that had her in its grip. 'I don't think I know what you mean.'

'Oh, come!' the older woman smiled gently, an understanding smile, but Liz had the impression of a cat, playing with a mouse. 'I've known Jean-Marc for a long time, and as you English say, the leopard doesn't change his spots.'

Fortunately for Liz, who hadn't been prepared for an outright attack, Berthe chose that moment to enter with a tray of coffee and croissants and while she poured herself a most welcome drink, Vivienne selected a cigarette, put it in a four-inch-long holder and lit it with a lighter which matched exactly the opulent-looking cigarette case. The door closed behind Berthe and Vivienne surveyed Liz through a cloud of cigarette smoke—it was a pitying look, and Liz felt the colour sweep into her cheeks.

'Yes, I see he has.' The pity was still there, but more in Vivienne's voice than in her eyes. 'He's very naughty, that one—but then he always was. I remember, when I first came to Villiers, I found him naughty too, but unlike you, I was very young. A well brought up girl, quite unused to men. He swept me off my feet so easily.'

Liz sipped her coffee and tried to look understanding and sympathetic. She reminded herself sternly it was quite possible that once upon a time Vivienne might have been unsophisticated, but looking at her now, Liz found that hard to believe. This woman, only a few years older than herself, had the appearance of being born knowing everything! On the other hand, Liz tried to be generous and fair-minded, she could be mistaken, she could be allowing her judgment to be swayed by personal prejudice, partly about the insinuation that she was neither young nor very well brought up.

Liz murmured without saying anything and waited for the next confidence. Vivienne was in a bosom-baring mood, there was more to come, for sure.

'I was very young, of course,' the older woman mused, 'and I think my head was turned by so much attention; not only from Jean-Marc but from the other young men in a small town like Villiers.' Vivienne gave a reminiscent smile as she let fall the hammer blow. 'We were lovers, you understand, Jean-Marc and I, and if he hadn't gone away to military service, I expect we should have been married, but he went away and forgot me. Oh, don't pity me!' Liz hadn't been going to, but on cue, she put on a pitying look.

'He was also young,' said Vivienne as though it was an excuse, 'and I suppose his new-found freedom went to his head. He didn't write or come home on his leaves, and naturally I knew I had to put him out of my mind. Then, after three years during which I didn't have even a postcard from him, I married his father. They were very much alike, you understand; Pierre was an older version of Jean-Marc and very kind. The sweetness of youth was no longer there, but I was very well satisfied. Pierre loved me madly, he bought this house for me—he said I was a jewel which deserved a better setting than that old farm.'

Liz nodded understandingly and sipped some more

coffee. She hoped the story wasn't going to be too long; after all, Vivienne had put across the important part, that she and Jean-Marc had been lovers. After that, nothing else needed to be said.

'Then, after four years away, Jean-Marc came home and I realised how great a mistake I'd made. We still loved each other, we knew that as soon as we met again.' Vivienne ground out her cigarette in a crystal ashtray and looked at Liz who, by this time, was feeling uncomfortable.

Perhaps she could have put up with a blow-by-blow account of a dead love affair at any other time but at breakfast. This was a story that would go down well at night when the lighting was soft and shadows collected in the corners of the room, it didn't belong in the bright light of morning—in any case, she didn't really want to hear it, but there was something about Vivienne's expression, about the whole attitude of her body, that told Liz she *was* going to hear it and a lot more besides, whether she wanted or not. This had been the reason for the seemingly casual meeting at the bottom of the stairs. Vivienne had been lying in wait for her.

'For two years nearly, we hid our love, Jean-Marc and I,' Vivienne said quietly. 'We were very discreet, but somehow or another, Pierre found out.' Liz felt the dark undercurrents sweeping her away to a kind of comic hysteria where it was all she could do not to laugh, but she crushed it all down behind a placid face and waited for the next instalment in silence.

'Of course, Pierre was very angry, but he didn't blame me, he knew his son better than anybody, and he did the only thing possible, he sent him away. Then Louis was born and Pierre and I were happy again until some years later, when Louis was nearly seven, Pierre had a heart attack—there was nobody else to help, nobody who would feel about Dieudonné as Pierre did, so he sent for Jean-Marc to come back and run things for him. This distressed me, you understand. I was afraid. . . . But my fears were unfounded. This time, Jean-Marc behaved in a most proper way. He was very hardworking, and gradually the rapport between him and his father was re-established, but it wasn't to last for long. Pierre had another attack, and this time it was too much for him, and he died.'

Liz murmured sympathetically. Perhaps with any other woman she would have reached out a comforting hand, but not with this one.

'But I must explain the present position,' Vivienne said firmly. 'My husband was an invalid for the last years of his life and the past preyed on his mind, so that when he died, there was only a small allowance for me, also one for Louis, and for Jean-Marc, there was, not the farm as he had hoped but the salary as a manager. Later, if he marries and has a son, that child will inherit it all, but if not, it will all go to Louis.' She gave a small, mirthless laugh. 'So you see, it all comes to the same thing in the end!'

'The same thing?' Liz felt the words being forced out of her; the undercurrent was icy cold and she could feel herself being swept away to somewhere dark and loathsome.

'Yes,' Vivienne whispered. 'But you must try to understand, Liz. Don't condemn us. What we did, what we still do, is wrong, but it's something we can't help, it's too strong for us—it always has been. Even now— not here, of course—but when Jean-Marc comes to Paris, there's nothing else we can do.' Tears welled into the huge dark eyes and Vivienne wiped them away with a minuscule scrap of lawn and lace. 'We can't marry and sometimes it's more pain than joy, especially now that he's taken my son away from me and brought him back here—he says this is right, the way it should be, but it breaks my heart. I've lost everything, my son, my husband, my home. . . .'

Liz registered shock involuntarily and Vivienne gave a pathetic little laugh, a laugh which held an element of shame. 'I've tried to break with him, but you understand, Louis is our link and I'm very weak. I still love Jean-Marc. Have I shocked you, Liz?'

Liz denied any shock, she *had* to. In any case, she wasn't feeling shock, only a sick distaste as though she'd turned over a clean, sunwarmed stone and found unpleasant things, dirty, pale worms, maggots and decomposition underneath it—things which would have been better left buried. Even allowing for Vivienne's rather histrionic way of telling her story, the peculiar, archaic phrasing which in other circumstances would have made her laugh, it was a slimy, disgusting little tale which bore no relation to the magnificence of Héloïse and Abelard.

She rubbed her hands down the sides of her jeans, as if to wipe away the soiled feeling from at least one part of her body, she felt physically sick and retreated into an icy remoteness.

'I can't think why you've told me all this, *madame*.' The steadiness of her voice surprised her, it also gave her confidence and she raised her chin. 'I'm merely a spectator. . . .'

Vivienne gave a hard, high little laugh. 'No, not a spectator, Liz. To be honest, I had word that Jean-Marc was up to his tricks again—little Marie-France, you know—a sweet child, she thinks she's in love with

him. Of course, she's years too young for him and he
will treat her gently because he knows it. She rang me,
I'm a friend of the doctor's and I think she thought I
might help her, but as soon as I realised that you might
be in danger, I came straight away. I felt you should be
warned.'

Liz pushed aside her coffee cup and rose. 'Thank
you, *madame*,' she was still wrapped in her ice. 'I also
am leaving today, I'm already packed, just a few things
more to put in my case and my car to fetch from the
farm. I wish you a pleasant journey back to Paris.' And
she walked steadily out of the room, although her knees
felt like cotton wool. There was only one thought in her
mind, that Jean-Marc and his stepmother were still
lovers—it was obscene, and then, as she reached the
foot of the staircase, her disgust turned into a violent,
raging temper.

She had called herself a fool last night. Fool was too
weak a word to use, she should have said 'cretin' or
'idiot' and anything else that was more descriptive. To
allow herself to be dragged into this disgusting little
mess—little mess was hardly a good enough phrase! She
thought if she scrubbed herself from head to toe with
disinfectant, she would never feel clean again!

Let him and Vivienne carry on with their dirty little
liaison, she was getting out before she became as
corrupted as they were. Now she could understand
Louis' uncertainty; children were very percipient, the
child probably had an idea of what was going on and
couldn't make head or tail of it, poor little thing.

For Vivienne and Jean-Marc she had no pity at all,
but for Louis, her heart wept. And to think she had
nearly succumbed to Jean-Marc's lovemaking! A
shudder shook her slender body and she went up the

stairs blindly, her eyes filled with tears of rage and self-disgust.

In her bedroom, she grabbed at the few things left hanging in the wardrobe and rammed them all into her case, paying no attention to her normal orderly way of packing. A couple of silk shirts, newly washed and exquisitely ironed by Berthe, were rolled up and stuffed into corners—they'd look a wreck when she took them out, but she didn't care. Halfway through stuffing in a bundle of underwear, a noise disturbed her and she went to the window to see Vivienne departing, her hairdo protected by a black chiffon scarf. The Porsche growled and then set off down the drive with a steady purr. So she was gone, and without a proper farewell to Louis; Liz sniffed derogatorily. That was supposed to be mother love? In her opinion, Vivienne was incapable of loving anybody but herself.

A gentle tap on the door distracted her just as she was leaning on her case, trying to get the lid shut and, without thinking, she yelled 'Come in', angry at being disturbed. She had been thinking about Ham, doubting whether she should leave him here in this place where the undercurrents were so dark and evil. But she couldn't expect a twelve-year-old boy to understand, not even if she explained in words of one syllable. In any case, how could she tell Ham a story like that, it wasn't fit for his ears.

The door opened and she didn't bother to turn round, supposing it to be the cleaning woman, so that when she heard Jean-Marc's voice, she spun swiftly to face him, her face a tight mask of distaste.

'You're packing?' He sounded surprised.

'Yes,' she said curtly, as she turned back to her case, rearranging a few things to make them lie flatter. She felt his hand at her waist and wrenched herself away as though she might be defiled by his touch. 'I'm leaving as soon as I've had a word with Ham. Are he and Louis back from the *piscine* yet?'

'Not yet—but why do you have to leave so suddenly?' and as she abandoned the packing and retreated, he advanced on her.

She took another pace backwards. 'Keep away from me, don't touch me!'

'Not touch you?' His eyebrows flew up. 'What's the matter, Liz?'

'What's the matter?' She echoed his question in a shrill voice. '*You* ask me what's the matter? I'll tell you! I've just had a most enlightening conversation with your *stepmother*,' she brought out the last word on an explosion of bitter derision. 'It wasn't so much a conversation as a blow-by-blow account of the last twelve years or so, and it wasn't so much enlightening as unpleasant. I feel as though I've fallen flat on my face in something filthy; that I'll never feel really clean again.'

'I see.' She watched while his face became once more that of a fallen angel, disillusioned, and the weary dead look came back to his eyes. He strode towards her until, backed up against the shutters of the window, she could retreat no further. 'You listen to poison and your mind absorbs it—to you, it's the truth. You don't ask for my side of it.'

'Why should I?' she flared, her face white and haggard. 'I prefer to rely on my own intuition, it's what I should have done all along. You see, I was right! I always thought this wasn't a good place for Ham to be, and I was right!'

'Ham! You pretend this is all about Ham?' he

snorted, and white patches of temper developed at the sides of his mouth and nose. 'You won't even be honest about that! This has nothing to do with the boy and you know it. I dragged you out of your shell and you resented it, so now you seize on any excuse to crawl back into your hiding place, even to believing Vivienne's lies, or pretending to. You shouldn't be out in the world, Liz, you should have walled yourself up in a convent, as safe from real life as you could get. . . .'

'There's no pretence!' Liz shouted back at him angrily. 'Vivienne told me the truth; no woman would make up a story like that. I saw her face while she was telling it, and I tell you, she was as ashamed of telling me as I was of hearing it!'

'Be quiet!' he shouted back at her. 'Do you want everybody to hear?

'Let them, I don't care,' she snarled. '*I've* done nothing to be ashamed of. Oh,' she gazed round her miserably, 'it's this house, this damn showplace—I've never liked it, and now I know why. It's full of sick decadence, and it's you and she who've made it so. No wonder your father sent you away, the miracle to me is that he ever let you come near him again! You seduced an innocent girl, and not content with that, you went and ignored her for years and then had the nerve to come back and have an affair with her while she was your father's wife. *And* I was quite right about Louis as well, he *is* your son—Vivienne admitted it! My God, how much lower can you get than that?'

'Oh, much lower!' Jean-Marc murmured softly while his eyes glittered with anger. 'There's something between us, Liz—would you like me to demonstrate just how strong that "something" is? And it's not only on my side. I was a fool that I didn't take you last night, you were crying out for it, despite all those protests about needing time. You wanted me as much as I wanted you and you can't deny it, but I had to play the hero, didn't I? Let the lady have the last word.'

Liz raised her chin scornfully. 'You're not irresistible, you know. You wouldn't have had it all your own way!'

'No?' His arms went round her and tightened until she could hardly breathe—she struggled against him and then went slack in his embrace. It wasn't any use struggling, it would only make matters worse, she knew that.

'Do what you like,' she said tonelessly. I haven't the physical strength to stop you. Go on, fling me down on the bed and get it over—and I wish you joy of it, because there won't be any joy in it for me. Or would you prefer the floor? That's a lot more primitive and you should get quite a kick out of it.'

For a moment he seemed to hesitate, she felt herself near to tears from the pain of her breasts crushed against his chest, and then his grip loosened and he held her lightly with one arm while his hand went to her cheek.

'No, Liz. Haven't I said I don't force any woman?' He had withdrawn mentally and his voice was as bleak as his face. 'We'll say goodbye and then you'll finish your packing. I'll phone the farm and have your car brought up, even if the paint's still wet. But you must delay long enough to say farewell to the boys—you know how important that is. And I don't want you to give them any hint of what's happened this morning. They mustn't suspect this is anything but a normal departure.'

'As if I would,' she muttered. 'What do you take me for, another Vivienne? I'll call for Ham on my way back, on the Saturday morning—we're booked on a night boat from Le Havre. I expect you could make arrangements to be busy on the farm or something. . . .'

'If that's what you wish,' and at her emphatic nod, 'but for now—we may never meet again, so allow me to say goodbye in my own way,' his smile was full of a bitter self-mockery. 'You can always wash yourself afterwards if you feel soiled by the contact.'

His hand ceased to caress her cheek and instead came to tip her face up to his. *'Au revoir, mignonne,'* he whispered, and his mouth found hers. There was a bitter-sweetness about that kiss and when he reluctantly raised his head, Liz found herself crying in earnest, the tears streaming down her cheeks unchecked.

She heard the door close behind him and stood quite still. It was a sound which had finality in it as though something very precious had been broken, and at last, thrown away as useless. With a trembling hand, Liz mopped at her streaming eyes and went on with her packing. And afterwards, when the case was finally closed and locked, she washed her face and redid it so that almost nothing showed, not her tears, not her aching heart, and she practised a gentle smile for the boys' benefit. But her eyes were as dead as Jean-Marc's.

# CHAPTER TEN

'WELL?' Marcie picked up her knitting and gestured with her head to the room above. 'We can talk now, Ham's asleep at last. Drat the boy, I thought he'd never drop off. What was it like in Avignon?'

'A desert.' Liz leaned back in her chair and wished she'd just dropped her nephew off and gone straight on to London instead of accepting her sister's invitation to stay. 'There wasn't anything there, if you see what I mean.' She glanced at the new watch she had bought herself and unwittingly smuggled through the Customs. It was a delicate, feminine thing, as unlike Bev's as she could find. When she got back to her own flat, she would root out a box and put her one earring and Bev's watch in it, together with the photographs, and she would put Jean-Marc in as well. 'I'm rather tired,' she murmured. 'Would you mind if I went straight to bed?'

'Oh no, you don't,' her sister said determinedly. 'You're not getting away like that! There's something different about you and I want to know what it is. You may as well tell me straight away, because if you don't, I shall nag you until you do!'

'Families are repulsive things,' Liz essayed a little humour. 'There's nothing different about me, it's all in your imagination.'

'Not so.' Marcie knitted furiously for a few minutes; she was halfway through a grey jumper, Ham-sized and looking as if it was part of school uniform. 'Come on,

Liz; you're looking as you did after Bev was killed, as though you'd lost the world and all.'

Liz dredged up some more humour, although she felt less humorous than she had ever done in her life. 'Alright, nosey, you ask the questions and I'll answer them—but only if I feel like it. If I don't feel like it, I shall be first cousin to a clam!'

Marcie snorted, knitted a few more stiches and then threw the needles and wool down on the couch beside her. 'I'll make an inspired guess,' she announced. 'It wasn't Avignon, so it must have been Dieudonné—and I think that means this Jean-Marc. Did you fall for him?'

Liz felt too tired, too empty for evasion. 'Please, Marcie, don't ask me. I don't want to talk about it.'

Her sister reached out a sympathetic hand. 'Ham said he was super, and coming from my son, that's high praise. What went wrong, my pet? Did he come on too strongly, or didn't he come on at all? I mean, did he make a pass or didn't he?'

'Yes,' Liz answered dully. 'He made a pass all right, but. . . .'

'. . . You passed it up? Oh, Liz, you are a fool! It would have been good for you.'

'Good for me?' Liz stopped being dull and sat bolt upright. 'Marcie, are you out of your mind? I never expected you to be advocating free love!' She made a poor joke of it. 'You wait until I see Ian, I'll tell him how low you've fallen!'

'A mind like a sewer,' her sister grinned. 'It comes of being nearly forty, one loses all one's inhibitions and one can't be shocked any more. Get it off your chest, Liz, and you'll feel better, you'll sleep better as well. You look as though you haven't slept properly for weeks, quite haggard, in fact—and don't blame it on the journey, I wouldn't believe you. Tell sister Marcie all about it, love; I can't bear to see you this way.'

With her eyes closed and the warmth of the fire on her face, Liz started to tell. She hadn't intended to tell everything, but somehow, leaving bits out made for chaos. She sat there in the quiet room for nearly twenty minutes and she talked steadily, leaving nothing out, not even Vivienne's story, and spoke as though repeating a book she'd read, dully and as if it had nothing to do with her. She went through it all from the time of the car crash until she had left for Avignon, and when she came to the end of it, she felt drained of everything, even pain.

'I think I love him,' she whispered. 'I didn't want to, I didn't mean to. He's not worth it, and I don't want a love like this—it hurts too much.'

Marcie had picked up her knitting and she finished the row before she spoke. 'Rather a long pregnancy, wouldn't you say—good enough for the Guinness Book of Records!'

'Umm?' Liz raised her head. 'That's a bit cryptic for me, please elucidate.'

'Jean-Marc and Louis, of course,' her sister said practically. 'Liz, you've been a married woman, yet you're still so damn innocent, you make me want to slap you!' Liz still looked mystified, and Marcie groaned. 'You say he was away, he'd been treated to the old "go and never darken my doors again" routine, that he was away for nearly ten years, yet when he came back, Louis was only seven. Now do you understand?'

'I could have made a mistake,' Liz hedged. 'After all, my memory's no better than anyone else's, and in any case. . . .'

'Three years!' Marcie scoffed. 'Sweetie, you've been had! That woman must be an eighteen-carat, gold-plated bitch, and if she lied about one thing, she'd lie about others. It's such an incredible story, I don't think I'd have believed a word of it. Maybe there's just a grain of truth there somewhere—perhaps they did have a thing going when they were young, but I'm willing to bet that kid's just what Jean-Marc said he was—his brother, and as for the rest, I'd need more than a pinch of salt to swallow all that undying passion thing. From what you've said, the woman's not the sort to inspire it.'

'He didn't deny it,' Liz shook her head, unwilling to be convinced.

'According to you, he didn't deny anything,' Marcie said briskly. 'And as far I'm concerned, that's a point in his favour.'

'About the only one, and as it's all over, I don't see the point in discussing it any more.' Liz rose to her feet and trailed gloomily off to bed.

Liz delayed her essay into life for several weeks until she found herself moping round her flat with too much time on her hands. Her box of memories had been put away, the past was over and she had the offer of a temporary post at the girls' school, to teach until Christmas. She didn't want to do it, but it offered an escape from four walls and her own thoughts.

Once there, she discovered she liked it; at least, everybody was alive and far too busy with their own affairs to bother about hers. The children were good for her as well and she got on well with them, even finding some pride in the way they seemed to like her and to improve under her tuition.

September drifted into October in a shower of

yellowing leaves and October into November, and before she knew it, everybody was talking about Christmas, starting to make plans and preparations. The bustle of shopping caught at her imagination and she spent hours deciding what to give Marcie and her family, choosing appropriate cards and having the odd evening out. People seemed to expect it of her, and in any case, sitting alone in the flat made her morose and even more unhappy. The pain had subsided to a dull ache which was always with her, even when she called herself a fool for feeling it.

She hadn't asked, she hadn't wanted to fall in love, but that sort of thing could happen to the most unlikely people and she, she reckoned, was the most unlikely of the lot. Gradually she was learning to stand on her own feet, make her own decisions; the past was gone and she had all the future in front of her. She wondered why she found no pleasure in that thought.

Marcie rang four days before Christmas. 'Louis has arrived and we're off to Wester Ross tomorrow. You won't be too lonely, will you?'

Liz didn't answer that one; instead she asked, 'Did you have to fetch him from the ferry?'

'No,' Marcie giggled. 'He was brought straight to the door by his brother—and I must say, my pet, you have very good taste. If it wasn't for Ian, whom I still love to distraction, I'd have fallen for Jean-Marc myself.'

'Did he stay long?' It was dreadful, this wanting to know every detail about him, and Liz flushed with shame at her need to just see him.

'Just the one night,' Marcie said coolly. 'He said he had to get back to work and he tells me he's moved down to the farmhouse. Poor man, I was sorry for him, all alone at Christmas, not even his brother for company.

Oh, by the way, I've received the things you sent and I'm mounting guard over them in case some itchy little fingers start tearing at the paper and spoil the surprise. See you the second week in January—you'll be able to spend a few days with us then, won't you?' and Marcie hung up while Liz nursed her injured feelings.

Her sister, her only sister, her only living relative, was sorry for Jean-Marc having to spend a lonely Christmas, but for herself, there'd only been a casual 'you won't be too lonely'. It wasn't fair, and after a solitary supper, she went to bed to brood about it. There'd been no message for her, not from Jean-Marc. He'd forgotten about her, and that wasn't fair either, not while she couldn't forget about him, not while the ache remained constantly with her.

Halfway through the night, she woke to a decision, not only about what she would do but what she felt. She was in love, and quite desperately so, she ached for fulfilment, and it didn't matter that the object of her love wasn't as stainless as a lily. Jean-Marc could be everything Vivienne had said and implied; she, Liz, didn't give two hoots. Maybe it was an unwise love, but she wasn't loving with her head, it was her heart and her whole body that loved him.

Black as sin or white as driven snow, Jean-Marc could be either, she didn't give a damn! And she would go to him and tell him so. It would be a humiliation if he rejected her, but humiliation would be better than this state of dull nothingness. She could get over rejection, it would be final, and she could turn another page and make another fresh start.

By this time it was breaking dawn, and she slithered out of bed, switched on the gas fire and made a cup of tea. Sitting with it on the rug before the fire, she made her plans. Marcie would be leaving early, trying to get as far north as possible on the first leg of the journey, maybe even as far as Inverness. Liz glanced at her watch and picked up the phone.

Marcie answered, sounding a bit harassed.'Oh, Liz, it's you—I thought for one dreadful minute Ian's leave had been cancelled again. Make it snappy, dear, we were just on the point of leaving—an early start, you know.'

'I'm going to France!' Liz announced.

'Oh?' Marcie didn't sound surprised. 'Clearing up unfinished business?'

'You could call it that,' Liz said dourly. 'I thought I'd better let you know in case you rang over Christmas.' A momentary thread of doubt struck her. 'I don't know if I'm doing the right thing. . . .'

'Does it matter? You're doing *something*, and that's always better than nothing, and if the mountain won't. . . . Good luck, little sister, have fun!'

'Luck!' Liz snorted. 'I'm going to need it!' and she hung up the phone and went to shower.

The Mini Traveller bounced happily down the minor road from Angers as though it knew that Calais, Paris, Orleans and Tours were behind it and it hadn't much further to go. It was just as dark and wet as it had been the first time, but tonight there was no gravel drive to turn into and no wind to blow trees in Liz's path.

The headlights illuminated the wrought iron gates of the mini-chateau and swept across a board that said, in big letters *'A Vendre'*. Liz smiled to herself. Somebody would come and buy it; a millionaire or business tycoon who wanted to make a splash and live in stately elegance, and she drove on by without giving it another thought.

As she turned the bonnet of the Traveller into the

farmyard, she started to tremble. Suppose there wasn't anybody there? Then she saw the light in the kitchen and breathed a sigh of relief. Somebody *was* there, possibly Berthe—perhaps Jean-Marc was out with a girl, all strictly lighthearted, brief and immoral. She grinned wryly to herself. A fine one she was to turn up her nose at immorality—after all, when all the cards were down, that was her purpose in coming here. All the same, she hoped he'd be in—her courage might evaporate during a long wait.

He answered her definite rap on the panels of the door and stood looking at her, neither smiling nor scowling. 'Liz?'

'Hullo,' she greeted him bravely. 'I hope you haven't got a houseful of guests, because I've come for Christmas.'

He stood back gravely, inviting her to come in, and she went past him into the kitchen, giving a little gasp of pleasure at the welcome warmth.

'What do you want, Liz?' He still wasn't smiling and there was a tight, hard line about his mouth.

'I'd like to get warm, have a cup of hot coffee and something to eat, in that order. I left London at some unearthly hour this morning,' she chattered on inanely, 'and except for an hour or so on the ferry, I've been driving ever since. When I left Orleans, something went wrong with the heater and my feet started to freeze— the process went upwards by stages, I think it's just about reached my knees. A fine welcome I get after driving part way across Europe—and I didn't bring you a Christmas present because I left in a bit of a hurry, but there'll be time to go into Angers tomorrow. . . .'

'. . . . Berthe's not here,' he interrupted. 'She's gone to stay with a friend in Saumur,' and at last, a smile curved his mouth. 'You can't stay here, Liz—you know what will happen.'

'Yes.' She raised clear, quiet eyes to his and what she saw there made her colour faintly. 'But that's what I came for, I'm counting on it!'

'And explanations?' He turned away to fill the coffee pot.

'Explanations,' she shrugged airily. 'Let's leave those till tomorrow, they're not all that important, are they?' Apparently she'd said the wrong thing, because his brows drew together and his voice had a hard, flat quality to it.

'Not important? Do you take me for a fool?' He put the coffee pot on the stove and swung round on her. His whole attitude, the expression or lack of it on his face, the way he held his body; it was all taut and inflexible, and for the first time, Liz felt despair uncoil within her. This wasn't going to be as easy as she'd thought in the flush of euphoric enthusiasm which had brought her here. She kept her eyes on his and waited for some sign of softening. It didn't come.

'Four months ago, you stormed out of that house,' his head jerked to indicate the general direction of the mini-chateau. 'After you'd told me just what sort of man you thought I was. Let's see if I can remember the details—and please tell me if I omit anything. I'd seduced an innocent girl and abandoned her, then four years later when I returned here to find her my father's wife. I carried on a guilty liaison with her until my father found out and banished me. I left the girl pregnant and allowed her to foist my bastard on my father, and then I stayed away until the old man was reduced to a bedridden invalid. Then once more I came back. . . .'

'. . . I don't believe Louis is your son,' Liz muttered an objection, all her confidence and euphoria drained away. Put the way he had put it, the tale seemed even more obscene; so much so, it was unbelievable, yet she *had* believed it. 'If this is the way you're going to behave,' there was a belligerent light in her eyes and her soft mouth firmed, 'don't bother about coffee or anything else. I'm leaving now!'

Jean-Marc's hand came hard on her shoulder, pushing her into a plain kitchen chair and pinning her there. 'Little fool, sit down and listen!' The grey of his eyes glittered like rims of polished steel round the black pupils. 'So you don't believe that part of the story—but it's only a very minor part. One small episode in nearly twenty years of vice which you think may not be true. Are you trying to tell me you forgive me the rest, that you've decided to be more than broad-minded about it, because that's what you'd need to be! What sort of woman are you, to turn a blind eye to such behaviour?'

'Let me go!' Liz twitched her shoulder; his grasp was becoming painful with his fingers tightening until the soft flesh gave way and she could feel them bruising against the bones.

'So you can run away again?' He shook his head, his face very close to hers as he bent over her. 'Oh, no, that's not the way it's going to be this time. You're not going anywhere, you're too tired to drive any more tonight, so I'm keeping you here until I get the truth from you, if it takes me until next Christmas.'

'I really can't spare the time.' From somewhere Liz found the spirit to drawl the words out mockingly and her chin raised with a faint assumption of hauteur. 'My sister's expecting me for the second week in January.'

'But you'll find the time.' Jean-Marc didn't unbend at all and she was suddenly afraid of this complete stranger she thought she had known. 'Come, tell me,' he continued smoothly, too smoothly, 'have you any concrete evidence that disproves my stepmother's romantic story?'

'None at all!' She wriggled against the pressure of his hands, becoming angry at the inquisition. 'Let's just say I give you the benefit of the doubt.'

'And forgive me my trespasses?' His smile was mirthless. 'That's not good enough.'

'Well, I can't do much more, can I?' she flared. 'You've never denied any of it!' She glared at him, her mouth set in a mutinous line. 'Oh, God! Why did I ever bother to come here?'

'And that's another question I'm asking,' he shot back at her. 'Why, believing what you do about me— why have you come? You, a pillar of purity, devoted to the memory of your dead husband, you come here—I tell you what'll happen if you stay but you aren't shocked or upset—instead, you behave like a *fille de joie*. That's not the impression you gave in the summer. The first time I kissed you, you were so frightened you ran away, and later, when I made a little restrained love to you, you said you liked it but anything more would make you ashamed of yourself. Why aren't you ashamed now? Have you been learning things over the past four months? What man has taught you that a live lover is better than a dead one, more satisfying than a memory? Has there been a man, Liz?'

'How dare you, let me *go*!' She struggled more fiercely against his grip, managing almost to free herself, but he shifted his hand and pushed her back ruthlessly in the chair. The hard back jarred against her

spine, making her gasp with pain, and tears started in
her eyes. None of this need ever have happened and she
couldn't think of one good reason why she had ever let
it happen. She'd been the most complete fool. . . .
Depression swept over her like a thick wet blanket;
extinguishing the fire of her temper to leave nothing but
a stale, acrid taste in her mouth.

'Why won't you deny those things Vivienne told me?'
she muttered sadly. 'You've only to say they're not true
and I'd believe you. . . .'

'And why should you believe me in preference to my
stepmother?' Jean-Marc brought his face closer to hers
so that she could see the deep, sardonic grooves on
either side of his mouth. 'There's no evidence for you to
pick over, it's just one person's word against another's,
so why believe me?'

It was all too much for her—the events of the day,
her hurried departure, the cold, bleak Channel
crossing—the long drive from Calais without food or
drink except for her milk, but through her cloud of
misery, a last spark of temper glowed.

'Because I love you, damn you!' She almost yelled it
in his face, and then her tears fell in earnest while she
bowed her head to hide this final humiliation. She felt
rather than saw the restraining arms being removed—
she heard him move away and there was the clatter of
china, the clink of a spoon in a saucer, but she still
didn't raise her head. He was a fiend! He'd nagged and
taunted her until she'd betrayed herself, and now he
would gloat over his conquest. Either that or he'd show
her the door, tell her he didn't want her and to get out.

'Coffee, Liz,' she raised her head at last, astounded at
the change in his voice and nearly stupefied with
weariness and shock. He wasn't harsh and cold any

longer, and she felt his hand gently stroking her hair.

'Don't pat me as if I was a stray dog,' she snarled, 'and don't be so bloody magnanimous either! What are you going to do now, graciously permit me to share your bed out of pity? I don't want pity and I won't have it. You've stood there like somebody in the gestapo, burrowing into my mind, probing for every last little thing. What have my motives to do with you? Why couldn't you have simply accepted? Why did you have to know everything? Why couldn't you have left me something?'

'Drink your coffee, *mignonne*.' Jean-Marc held the cup to her lips as though she was a very young child, unable to hold it. Her nose wrinkled distastefully at the smell and she pushed it away.

'You've put brandy in it—I can't drink that—and there's another thing. I've meant to tell you before. Don't call me by that stupid name. *Mignonne!*' she snorted disparagingly. 'That means sweet and dainty, and that I'm not.'

'Drink!' Once more the cup was pushed against her lips. 'You need it—and you'd better start learning a little about French marital relationships. A woman has her kitchen, but in matters of her comfort and wellbeing, she defers to her husband.'

'Marital relationships!' Liz took a sip, and gasped as liquid fire ran down her throat. It settled in her empty stomach with a warming glow and she discovered what 'Dutch courage' really meant. 'Who said anything about marital anythings? I certainly didn't, I've never mentioned them. I don't think I want to marry you anyway, you're not my idea of an ideal husband by any means.' She drank the rest of the coffee in one gulp and felt the glow spread through the rest of her body to set her fingers and toes tingling.

'We can discuss that later.' Jean-Marc sounded amused as he hauled her from the chair. 'Come and share my supper. Berthe, before she left, filled the fridge with cooked things that could be reheated. Tonight it's a quiche, and it should be ready by now.' He drew her into his arms to divest her of her fur jacket and, in passing, his mouth found hers.

It was worth waiting for, Liz decided muzzily as she softened against him, letting the jacket fall to the floor unheeded. If he'd done this as soon as she'd come in, they'd have saved a lot of time! Her hands went up to hold his head down to hers and her mouth grew greedy under his, her lips parting at his insistence. When he raised his head at last, his whole face was softer and his eyes, beneath their heavy lids, were hardly showing any grey at all, the black irises distended and little yellow flames flickering in the darkness.

'Later,' he murmured. 'Set the table, *ma mie*, while I get the dish from the oven.'

Love, Liz discovered, could wait for a little while; just at present, hunger was more important, and she cheerfully rattled among the wall cupboards for plates to warm.

'Are the cupboards the right height for you?' he enquired.

'They could have been tailor-made.'

'They were,' but she pretended not to hear him, going instead to help herself to another cup of coffee. She eyed the cognac bottle wistfully, but decided against it, although the glow was beginning to fade from her stomach and she was feeling apprehensive about what she was going to do. It was fine while his arms were about her and his mouth on hers, then she didn't care about anything, but away from him, she could feel uncertainty growing, chilling her blood and sending her heart racing.

Jean-Marc brought the quiche to the table to cut her a generous slice, and she took a seat and looked at it while the rich, savoury aroma attacked her nostrils. Her stomach protested against the lean diet she had been feeding it and she could feel her mouth watering. Unconsciously, as she picked up her fork, she licked her lips, and it made him chuckle.

'Don't bother about making polite conversation, Liz. You look famished!'

She needed no second invitation, she stuffed a forkful into her mouth, chewed and then spoke through the crumbs of Berthe's incomparable pastry. 'I am. Milk may be nourishing and sustaining, but it doesn't give you that lovely full feeling!'

'And you had only milk?'

'Mmm.' She didn't raise her eyes from her plate until it was empty. 'I thought it would save time,' and she eyed what was remaining on the dish. 'May I have some more, please, it's not your lunch tomorrow or anything like that, is it?'

'No, tomorrow we have pâté for lunch and a roast chicken for dinner, and since you'll be here to cook it, I'll bring in a capon for Christmas Day.'

'I'm not much of a cook,' Liz reminded him. 'I told you once before, I've never had much practice.'

'You'll learn, I'll buy you a cook book.' He waved aside her doubts and watched as her second helping disappeared from her plate less swiftly than the first, and she beamed at him with contentment.

'That was *good*, and I feel miles better; shall we have that talk now?'

'Mmm, but not here,' he looked around the shining kitchen. In the *salon*—it'll be more comfortable and there's an electric fire if the central heating isn't warm enough for you.'

'Can't you, won't you explain?' Liz almost whispered as she seated herself on the couch. She was suddenly afraid his smile would go, to be replaced by his former enigmatic expression. 'Do you know what your stepmother told me?'

'Within limits.' He came to sit beside her, putting an arm about her, which gave her a little more courage. 'She's told the story several times with small variations, mostly to a girl or woman if she thought I was showing an interest in that quarter. She has somebody in Villiers who tells her what I'm doing.'

Liz thought of green eyes filled with malice and shuddered away from it. 'Then you could have told me the truth months ago.'

'What's the truth, *ma mie*?' Jean-Marc felt in his pocket for cigarettes and lit one while he stared at the glowing bars of the fire. 'Truth is what one believes, and Vivienne's told the story so many times, she's believing it herself. That's why it sounds so good, she gives it a genuine ring of authenticity. In several details, she's quite correct—before I went to the army, we were lovers—but I didn't seduce an innocent maiden, you must believe that.'

'She said you went away, that you never wrote. . . .'

'. . . and that is also a point where our stories agree, it's true, for both of us, but she gave you no reason, and that's where we start to differ. Do you want to hear my side?'

'If you don't tell me, if you insist on sitting silent while everybody is allowed to think the worst of you, I'll throttle you!' threatened Liz, a militant sparkle in her eyes.

He caught the glint of it and chuckled. 'What a

warlike lady I'm going to marry—but it's quite simple, *ma chérie*. I was a very young man, I was in love and I asked the girl to marry me. But like the wise, sensible girl she was, she refused! Me, I was heartbroken and disillusioned at being told I couldn't afford to keep a wife in the manner to which my love wished to become accustomed—that she deserved something better than a glorified farm labourer, and that was what I was, only not as well off as other farm labourers. My father was thrifty, he housed and fed me and gave me pocket money out of which I had to buy my clothes. Vivienne turned up her nose at such a poverty-stricken swain, and the promise that one day he would inherit the farm didn't make her relent. That was too long a wait, and besides, she wasn't fond of hard work. She would have had the care of two men in a house without a single modern convenience.' He smiled at her gently.

'Can you blame her?' he continued. 'So, bitter and full of frustrated love, I went off to the army. I was young and romantic and I wanted a war somewhere so that I could be killed and she would weep for me, but there were no wars, and after my training, I volunteered for the Legion, where several sergeants and officers swiftly rid my mind of sentimental rubbish.'

'And when you came home at last, she'd married your father.'

'Another point where we agree, but after that. . . .' he shrugged. 'Papa didn't discover an illicit liaison because there wasn't one. His new wife was now my stepmother, and in any case, I'd grown out of my infatuation. But Vivienne doesn't like it when her victims escape, she redoubles her efforts to recapture them. I stood it as long as I dared and then, like a coward, I ran away.' He grinned at her wryly. 'I'm neither a saint nor a monk, and I thought it safer to have a lot of miles between us, although I'll admit, if she'd been anybody else's wife . . . but not because I was in love with her. It was just that it would be somebody else if it wasn't me. . . . My going made my father angry, I'd been home for nearly two years and he'd come to rely on me—he was getting old and, worse still, he had to employ a man in my place to do the clerical work.' Jean-Marc dropped into silence and Liz had to prompt him.

'Go on.'

He shrugged again. 'Papa had a heart attack that finished him as an active man and he sent for me to come home. By this time I thought I could handle it; ten years away, a bit of sophistication and a wider knowledge of the female sex—it all helped. In any case, I had no time for dalliance. Louis was nearly seven, the farm was run down to provide money for Papa's young wife—Papa was ill and old, but although he was still very much in love with her, he was no fool. He knew things weren't as they should be and he wanted to make Dieudonné safe for the future. That's why I'm only the steward, Vivienne, foolishly, had told him of our brief love affair once when they were quarrelling, and he was afraid I'd be as generous to her as he was, so he made it impossible before he died.'

'She said something to me about only having an allowance,' Liz murmured. 'I wasn't in any state to take it in, though. . . .'

'No,' he pulled her against him. 'I can understand that. But, I was never her lover after she became my stepmother, that's *my* truth! When I came back the second time, I disliked and despised her. She'd nearly ruined a prosperous farm with her extravagance and she was driving my father to his death with her constant demands. After he died, I found there was no money left except the profits from the farm, which just about covered the allowances and paid the wages bill. We had to abandon our own winemaking and join the co-operative, and I used some money I'd had from my mother's people in Normandy to buy new stock and machinery. With that, Dieudonné survived, but it was a very close thing—it still is!'

'Jean-Marc,' there were tears in her eyes and she seized his hand, 'I'm sorry. Will you ever forgive me?'

'Forgiving doesn't enter into it.' He pulled her closer, lifting a finger to smooth away her tears. 'I love you, Liz. I loved you that first night when I carried you into the house.'

'And you didn't make a good impression,' she giggled, 'letting trees fall in my way so that I'd crash!'

'But I brazened it out,' he murmured in her ear. 'I even made you apologise for thinking badly of me. But what about the past, your past? Are you still clinging to it?'

'No,' she shook her head firmly. 'I've put it away, which is what I should have done ages ago.'

'And you'll marry me, although you'll be starting with a readymade family and we shan't have a lot of money?' Jean-Marc pulled her round to face him. 'There'll be enough, of course, we shall be quite comfortable, but I can't allow Louis to live with his mother,' he grimaced. 'She has a life style which confuses a child.'

Liz absorbed the implication and dismissed it. Vivienne's life-style had no importance for her— Vivienne herself wasn't important, not any longer. 'I've never had a lot of money,' she said dreamily, 'so I shan't miss it, and Louis and I get on well together. As for the rest,' she smiled up at him. 'the answer's yes. Whenever and wherever you like; I was hoping you'd ask me again.'

'Then, since you've been fed, all that remains is to find you somewhere to sleep. We've a couple of spare rooms, but I don't recommend Louis', he has an orthopaedic mattress which will be too hard for you.'

Liz looked at him primly while her eyes twinkled. This was her own dear man, and with him she'd touch the stars. 'Fetch my case in from the car,' she suggested, 'while I go and view the accommodation on offer, although it sounds as if I'll have a very limited choice.'

Jean-Marc made no move to go, instead his mouth found hers and she felt the power of the dark current sweeping her away, but this time she made no resistance as she felt herself being carried along. Her mouth parted and her slender body arched against him, her hands seeking, almost tearing, until there was smooth warm skin under her fingertips.

'A very limited choice,' Jean-Marc raised his head and spoke huskily. 'Either alone or with me.'

'Which is no choice at all,' she said softly. 'Why do you think I came all this way, and like I said before, I'm counting on it, so you needn't bother about getting my case, not until tomorrow morning. *Filles de joie* don't bother about things like that, do they?'

'My acquaintance with those ladies is small,' he smiled at her aggravatingly as he rose and picked her up in his arms, 'but being French and very practical, I can't let you do something like this on the spur of the moment.' He set her on her feet and held her away from him. 'Liz, are you sure this is what you want?'

'Uhh?' She looked up at him in surprise. 'I thought we'd been into all that!'

'Yes, we have, *chérie*, but,' he held her firmly for a second and then his arms dropped and he stood back, 'I have to make you see—You came to me. It had to be that way, do you understand? But you once said you'd be ashamed and that it would spoil things for both of us, and I don't want that. I want everything to be perfect for us. We shall have the rest of our lives together, and I can wait a few more days if you think that would be better. We can have Christmas together and then go to England and be married—they do things more quickly there than in France. I haven't much to offer—I don't want you to do one thing you might regret—I can wait. . . .'

'Silly!' Liz took the step forward that would take her back into his arms and put her hands up to his face, holding it tenderly while she raised herself on her toes and gently kissed his mouth. 'I love you, Jean-Marc. I came because I love you. I'm not the least bit ashamed. I want to be with you, nothing else matters.'

'You're sure?' His arms were about her once more. 'Because once I have you, I'll never let you go, you know that. You'll live the rest of your life with me, there'll be no escape. . . .'

'I know,' murmured Liz. 'A fate worse than death.' She gave a watery chuckle as she realised he probably wouldn't understand the implication. 'Oh, my darling,' she drew his head down to hers, 'there'll be no shame, no regret, not for me, not ever. Nothing can spoil what we have.'

She watched the dark, closed look leave his face and a smile, as young and mischievous as Louis', curve his lips; her dear Lucifer had struggled free of his hell, and together they would both find heaven.

'In that case, *madame*,' his arms shifted their hold to sweep her off her feet, 'I need no other invitation. I think we've both wasted enough time!'

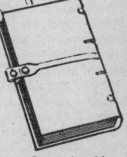